ANGELA C. CHARLES

RELINQUISHED

INSPIRED BY A TRUE STORY OF RESILIENCE AND HOPE

ISBN: 978-1-4866-2669-4
eBook ISBN: 978-1-4866-2670-0

Word Alive Press
119 De Baets Street Winnipeg, MB R2J 3R9
www.wordalivepress.ca

WORD ALIVE
—P R E S S—

Cataloguing in Publication information can be obtained from Library and Archives Canada.

Angela C. Charles did it again and executed another brilliant piece of writing. An extraordinary journey through the depths of rejection, pain, resilience, and courage, which offers readers several moments of profound connection and inspiration.

—Amanda J. Edwin, B.Ed (Hons), MSc

Writer Angela C. Charles guides us through Nikki's journey with honesty and empathy. Nikki's voice gives the reader unique insights into a teenager who finds herself outside of the normal school system and "acceptable" society. Nikki's traumatic experiences never overshadow who she is and who she will become.

—Anandi Carroll-Woolery, Chair, Afric-Caribbean Book Club Waterloo Region

Hope Relinquished is an unflinchingly honest and profoundly moving narrative that delves into the depths of human suffering and resilience. Angela C. Charles masterfully tells a story filled with pain, trauma, depression, acceptance, migration, the need to fit in, and the harrowing realities of rape and teenage pregnancy. The protagonist journeys in a culture and country unfamiliar from what she has known until her teenage years. Her heart-wrenching secret is depicted with raw authenticity and emotional depth.

This book is not just a story but a testament to the strength of the human spirit. The characters are so vividly drawn that their struggles and triumphs resonate long after the last page is turned. *Hope Relinquished* is a must-read for anyone seeking a deeper understanding of the complexities of trauma and the enduring power of hope and healing. Angela has crafted a powerful and unforgettable tale that will leave readers both heartbroken and inspired. It's a poignant reminder of the resilience within us all and the importance of facing our truths, no matter how painful they may be.

—Veronica Jubénot-Shillingford, BABM, BScN, NP-PHC, MD

TO ALL THE mothers who made the difficult choice to place their babies for adoption, and those who had no choice: You may never find the answers you're looking for or see the face of the absent child. Pain, loss, and guilt might always surround you. May you find peace and healing.

To all the adopted children: You may never find your birth mother, make the connection you desire, or find the answers you're looking for. But I pray that a happy childhood and loving adoptive parents were enough to give you closure.

CHAPTER
ONE

"Of all the hardships a person had to face, none was
more punishing than the simple act of waiting."
—Khaled Hosseini, *A Thousand Splendid Suns*

OUR BATHROOM IS small, safe, and unoccupied. Just the right amount of
space I need for a hideaway. Unfortunately, the summer heat is turning it into
a steam room, making my skin wet. Moisture covers the small mirror, trick-
ling down the walls, leaving streaks in its wake as the beads join together to
run slowly and steadily in a small stream on the floor. My clothes stick to my
small frame, and my normally curly hair is frizzy, with a few drenched strands
resting against my cheeks. Most people use steam baths for therapeutic
reasons. However, sitting in this place has more to do with my questionable
sanity than with health reasons.

So here I am, crouched down on the floor with hunched shoulders, rock-
ing back and forth, clutching my fists so tightly that the nails bite into the
flesh of my palms. Added to that, the unbearable heat wraps around me like
a blanket, causing sweat to run down my body, beading on my forehead. I'm
reduced to a bundle of nerves.

Opening a window is the last thing on my mind. Within this small space,
the ticking sound from the small travel clock, perched on the edge of the
bathroom sink, reverberates like the sounds of Big Ben, the great clock in
London, heralding every second.

Letting out a deep sigh, I know with certainty that this will turn out to be the longest five minutes in my young life. I shift uncomfortably. Fear, worry, and anxiety intensify the sweat running freely down my face and back. My heart hammers. It feels loud in my ears. *Thump. Thump. Thump.*

My breathing increases. I squint. However, with a will of their own, my eyes remain locked on the tiny device in front of me. A simple dipstick with the power to tell the direction of my life. My lips move, but no sound comes out. Is this how a prisoner feels awaiting her fate? I briefly look up a few inches above the device to see innumerable specks of dust on the floor. Inconsequential. The wait becomes like that found in a suspense movie. One where tense anticipation drives you to the edge of your seat, causing you to clench your stomach muscles so tightly that they ache and your head spins with a million scenarios as you wait for the door to open, as you help-lessly wait for the reveal. Nothing else matters. My anxiety rises. And just like a suspense or horror movie, I imagine what will happen to me. Fear crowds me, causing my mind to become stuck in a loop of anxious and confusing thoughts, spinning out of control.

Four minutes.

I breathe in deeply in fearful anticipation. I should have gone to that psychic reader. Maybe. I saw the sign on the door when I took a shortcut on my way to school. The neon sign promised accurate readings in minutes. The tarot cards or whatever instrument the reader used would tell my future in less than five minutes, and it would certainly be less nerve-racking. When I was twelve years old, I read somewhere that fortune tellers used crystal balls and cards to predict a person's future in little or no time.

In my case, the psychic reader only had two options no matter which card she drew. That meant she didn't even need five minutes. One card would mean I turn right on the paved road with lessons learned, settle down, and continue living as a normal teenager. The other card would predict I had to turn left along the narrow dirt path and live with the consequences. What card would she draw? Which road led to my future?

But now, sweating profusely, I'm standing at what feels like the fork in the road. Waiting. My heart beats faster. My breath comes out in short gasps.

Three minutes.

CHAPTER ONE

Salty droplets run down my face, remaining suspended for a few seconds before dribbling onto the floor. Time moves at a snail's pace. Five minutes seems like an eternity. My lips move. "Please, Lord. Please! Am I not a good person? I tried my best to be one. I always remember to say 'please' and 'thank you.' A year ago, I found it easy to be kind to people. But now it's hard. So awfully hard. Still, I think I'm a good person, although sometimes I fail. Don't you think so? I'm so sorry for fighting with Mikey. But you know that was my only fight. I didn't mean to hit him. But what could I do? He called me a cry-baby. I like Mikey. He was my friend. I'm sorry. Don't punish me. Please!"

Silent tears join with the sweat rolling down my face. I mumble, asking forgiveness for all the perceived crimes I committed and for any future crimes.

Two minutes.

My heart feels like a jackhammer now with its pounding. I feel the pulse under my fingertips throbbing in tune with the racing of my heart. I break out in a cold sweat. Desperation colours my words. "I'll be good, Lord. What do you want me to do? I'll do whatever you want me to do. Anything. I'll do my homework on time. I won't give my mother any trouble. I'll try to like the people at school. I promise not to hit anyone else. I'll be good. I'll do anything. Just don't let it be you-know-what. I messed up. Bad. I'm scared. Scared of knowing. Scared worse than when I had to wait for the nurse to give me that tetanus shot. Back then, I could only remember the darkness and thinking I wouldn't live to see my seventh birthday."

I have a headache. My head is throbbing. My thoughts become chaotic and negative, focusing on the results and the inconceivably life-changing consequences to follow.

How will I survive? Can I survive? I know I will just die. Maybe the wait will kill me first.

One minute.

I rub my sweaty palms together in an attempt to keep from hyperventilating, to keep from freaking out. But with only one minute to go, any hope for a reprieve vanishes. Too late. Is my future sealed? Is one minute enough time to change fate? Maybe begging might change the outcome. "Please, Lord, don't let it be what I think. Can you change the hand that I'm dealt? Can you change my fate?"

My stress reaches an all-time high. I suck in air, and my eyes widen. The room suddenly darkens as the sun disappears behind the clouds. I gasp and start to tremble. I'm certain it forebodes something cataclysmic. I hear the whisper of the old folks' voice in my ear: "Little Nikki Robinson, you're going to hell in a handbasket." My stomach tightens in knots until it aches. I bend forward, wrapping my arms around my body, biting my lower lip, hoping to disappear into the floor or wake up from the nightmare. My eyes grow wide as saucers.

Zero. Time has run out. The five minutes has expired.

Lord, help me!

My breathing becomes fast and shallow, and I breathe out. I begin to shake, then place one hand on the floor to keep me steady while slowly extending my other trembling hand. I hold my breath, subconsciously noticing the shimmer of moisture on my brown arm in contrast to the white-knuckled fist reaching for the dipstick. The colour band that will reveal the answer and predict my future. I freeze in terror, my mouth is dry, and my mind goes blank.

Positive.

Darkness descends.

CHAPTER
TWO

"Shame hates it when we reach out to tell our story. It
hates having words wrapped around it – it can't survive
being shared. Shame loves secrecy ... When we bury our
story, the shame metastasizes."
—Brene Brown, *The Gifts of Imperfection*

MY EYELIDS FLICKERED then opened wide with awareness. *Oh Lord*. My
heart skipped a beat then started speeding up like a runaway freight train.
My worst nightmare! Pregnant. The reality of what the word meant slammed
into me with such force that it pushed me away from the instrument. I wanted distance. Grabbing the front of my t-shirt with trembling hands, I hoped
to still my racing heart, hoped to keep it from turning into a frog and jumping
out of my chest. Looking at the colour band on the dipstick, I saw the mouth
of a venomous snake. A snake whose bite brought new life. And death.
Death to my dreams. I leaned back. Afraid to move. Afraid to faint again.
Afraid to think of the word. Yet it turned into an endless song. I closed my
eyes but was unable to shut it off. Shut off the chant. The world tilted. I found
myself at the top of a mountain. A desolate place with no clearing or trails to
walk, no ropes to rappel down.

A cascade of tears mixed with my heavy sobs as I released the entire
weight of my fear with the devastating force of a category five hurricane.
In my short lifetime, I hadn't lived through a devastating hurricane, but as
part of hurricane preparedness, we learned that catastrophic damage would

occur afterwards. Tears started to flow down my face like the rain in a tropical thunderstorm.

I moaned while I rocked back and forth, wrapping my arms around my
middle. "No, no, no. Lord, help me!" I called on a God I knew with my head,
not my heart. The moan grew louder. "Why? Why did this happen? I'm dead.
My ... mother ... will ... kill ... me."

The pain in my heart intensified, causing another flood of tears at the
thought of what awaited me. I whispered, "I'm so ashamed. What do I do?
Oh Lord, how will I face everyone?" I hugged the back of my knees. My
shoulders heaved.

A few minutes later, with tremendous effort, I stood leaning against the
sink, mopping my face, grateful not to see my reflection in the clouded mirror. A mirror with an old crack. Was I not just as cracked and broken like the
mirror? The mirror would be replaced in time. *But what about me?* What
happened to people like me who made mistakes? A dumb choice but one
with no second chances. Tears distorted my vision, and my nose ran as I
staggered toward my bedroom pressing my hand to my aching chest.

I touched the handwritten sign on the door. A gift from my sister, Valerie,
which said "Princess Nikki," but in my guilt I saw "Pregnant Nikki." Shame
rose and infused my body from head to toe. I stumbled. It was as though a
hurricane smashed into my life, obliterating the future I dreamed of and for
which I'd planned. I took a step into my bedroom, blinked, and for a second
I stood at the edge of darkness. With no other choice, I stepped into the dark
unknown, my young life suddenly shattered and divided by Before and After.

The shock from the revelation left me bewildered. I peeled off the wet
clothes and wrapped the sheet around me before sitting on the edge of the
bed to stare lifelessly into space. My fourteen-year-old voice resonated with
despair, anguish, and disbelief. "Why? Why did this happen? I don't want
to be pregnant. I didn't choose to get pregnant." My voice broke. "I'm too
young to be pregnant. I'm still a child!" Dry sobs racked my body, plunging
me into despair.

I only wanted a friend, not a baby.

Exhausted, I dropped into bed, curled into a ball, and fell asleep.

• • •

I heard my mother's voice about an hour later. "Nikki, I'm home."

I rolled over and groaned aloud. "Oh Lord! I'm dead. For sure!" I sat on the edge of the bed, wrestling with all the questions, anxiety, and confusion that clouded my mind.

I wish I could run away.

But where would I go? Words sprang to my lips as I tried to hold back the wail rising from deep within me. "I wish I would shrivel up and die. I wish I had never come to this country," I said, hoping that my mother didn't hear me. I put my head in my hands. "What shall I do? Do I tell her or not? How I wish the ground would open and swallow me. Lord, help me."

Courage, Nikki, courage.

Every step was leading me to a future that scared me witless. My life had just turned into a bleak and lonely place—a place I didn't want to explore. My voice broke as I spoke my thoughts out loud. "Now I have secrets. But for how long? How long can I hide? What price will I have to pay?"

The road in my young life had suddenly taken an unexpected turn. I had run out of options. I didn't have a choice but to live with the consequences. One thing I knew for sure was that the place I would end up was not the one of which I had dreamed.

"Hi, Mama." I plastered a smile on my face, keeping my gaze on the food laid out on the table.

My mother, Marian, dressed in a casual floral-print summer dress with an open neck and short sleeves, stood at the kitchen counter with a cup in her hand. She glanced over her shoulder. "Nikki! Finally! I was about to check on you. Child, what took you so long?"

I fanned my face with one hand. "It was hot. I must have dozed off."

My mother drained the contents of the cup and placed it in the sink before turning and leaning against the counter. "It's going to be a hot August. You keep forgetting to adjust the air conditioner." She shook her head in exasperation. "Do you remember how to adjust it?"

Why does she always think I'm stupid?

"Yes, ma'am. But I didn't put it on. I don't mind the heat." I took a deep breath before looking at the floor, ashamed of the flare-up of unexpected anger. However, I knew she wouldn't notice I was short with her. "You brought dinner. Thanks."

Hope I don't vomit.

My mother straightened her tall frame, picked up a bowl with her other hand, and walked with smooth, relaxed steps to the table. My sister, Val, and I have a standing joke that our mother would die of a heart attack if she even gained five pounds.

My mother sucked her teeth. "You're just like your father. He also preferred the sweltering heat to the cool air."

Better him than you.

My mother shook her head then ran a smoothing hand over her permed hair pulled back in a bun. "Anyway, I can't be bothered cooking tonight. I have an early date." A dreamy look appeared on her face as she placed the bowl on the table before sliding into one of the chairs. "This is for you and Eli. I've already eaten. Hope you're hungry."

I grabbed a glass of water before sitting across from my mother and taking a sip. "Burger with fries." Another sip. "Looks good."

My mother munched on one of the fries. "Nothing fancy. I figured you wouldn't mind, since we're eating out tomorrow," she said, giving me a huge smile. "It's your big day. I'm looking forward to celebrating your birthday. Fourteen years! Did I tell you where we're going?"

"Ahh … no."

She continued. "I didn't? Anyway, we're going to a restaurant that offers comfort food and island cuisine. My friend George told me about it. He highly recommends the Saturday brunch." An enigmatic smile appeared on her face.

I added a few fries with my burger. "Just us, right?" referring to my brother, Eli, and my sister, Val.

Marian shifted in her chair. "I invited George." My mother had recently started dating, spending all her free time with George Plummer.

"Oh! Okay, I guess. Anyway, I'm looking forward to seeing Val. I don't get to see much of her since she moved to Toronto."

She frowned. "Nikki, you know Valerie can't drive from Toronto every weekend to see you. She has her own life."

"I didn't expect …"

Glaring at me with narrow, dark-brown eyes, my mother interrupted me. "Oh for Pete's sake! That's another thing. You know I don't like it when you call her Val. I've never liked that nickname. She has a perfectly suitable name." My mother always called my brother "Eli," conveniently forgetting she had given him the perfectly suitable name of Elijah.

I took a bite of the burger and chewed.

My mother shook her head. "You made me lose my train of thought. Oh yes, Valerie. She has to be careful. I'm so happy she's pregnant. Naturally, the baby is her first priority."

She's pregnant, not dying!

My thought might have reflected on my face because my mother changed her tune.

"Anyway, this trip is special." My mother sighed, focusing her gaze on a spot beyond me. "You should be thankful that she's making it for you."

I said something unintelligible, which my mother ignored.

"I told George how much I'm looking forward to my first grandchild. Do you know what he said?" She waited, but I suddenly took an interest in my food. She gushed. "He said that he was certain I wouldn't be one of those mothers who exert pressure on their children to produce a grandchild. He says the sweetest things. Don't you think so?" Her sigh came out like a soft breeze.

I concentrated on nibbling the burger, chewing, swallowing, and hearing without listening.

Suddenly her voice rose. "You wouldn't guess what I bought," she said, stretching her hand under the table to retrieve a bag.

I was so wrapped up in my shame that I hadn't noticed a bag under the table. A spark of hope. Was it the dress I wanted? My mother couldn't have missed all the hints I'd dropped for weeks. Plastering on a smile, I sat up straighter, prepared to open my gift. My mouth opened, but the words remained stuck in my throat when she reached into the bag. "Voila! Here it is!" she proclaimed, producing a small blanket with a flourish. "What do you think?"

I closed my mouth, unable to hide the disappointment or ignore the hurt in my heart.

"Do you like it?" My mother rattled on, not even waiting for an answer. "I saw this in the store and couldn't resist." She smiled, resting her gaze on the blanket. "Isn't it adorable?" She pressed it against her face, a shade lighter than mine, before returning it to the bag. "I know. I know. I'm going to spoil this baby."

I threw away the half-eaten burger while my mother was still gazing adoringly at the blanket. "I'm going to bed early tonight. Big day tomorrow!"

"Sure, honey." My mother looked down at the bag. "I think I'll sign the card as Glamorous Grannie. How does that sound?"

I didn't answer. Secrecy and shame warred within me. I left the room listening to my mother repeating the name "Glamourous Grannie." When I had almost reached the door to my bedroom, my mother called out, "I'll sign your name on the card."

I leaned against the closed door with tears pouring down my face, my heart breaking into a million pieces as I muttered, "Sign it how? As Pregnant Aunty?" Shame gripped me unrelentingly.

CHAPTER
THREE

"The past was filling the room like a tide of whispers."
—Ross Macdonald, *The Instant Enemy*

I FLOPPED ONTO my comforter and stared at the ceiling. How did I get to this place? This place of shame. There was no one to talk to, no one to help me. Alone even when my mother was home. I was glad she was going out. Closing my eyes, I called to mind the week I came to live in Canada with my family, away from the island of Dominica, where I was born and lived until then. But truthfully, loneliness had started creeping in two years earlier when my siblings joined our parents in Canada, leaving me to live with my aunt on the island. Abandoned at age eleven.

Eleven months ago, I had arrived in Canada with mixed emotions. Thrilled to be reunited with my siblings but hurt that I wouldn't be with my father, whom I adored. Knowing that my father had left my family made me sad. Even though I hadn't seen him in some time, I would miss him because I was closer to him than my mother, always. He was in Toronto and my mother was in another city, not like I could visit him easily. The closeness I shared with him had made up for my strained relationship with my mother.

In addition to my emotional upheaval, everything in Canada became a new experience. I recalled shivering while shopping with my mother a week after I arrived. She had scolded me. "For the love of Mike! Stop crossing your arms. It's not that cold." She exhaled deeply when I slipped on the warm coat. "Okay. Let's get some more warm clothes. I think you'll need them right away."

• • •

My life had continued to unravel. Bereft of everything I knew, my world became a chaotic place, leaving me frightened and confused. I had difficulty getting settled from my first day at the junior high school, two weeks later. Instead of feeling comfortable with my environment, it felt like the earth beneath me had started to shift.

Or maybe I was the one who shifted. I remembered standing rooted on the spot. Then I had turned my head to watch the classroom door close. My mind went blank for a minute before a vision of the most recent landslide on the island of Dominica flashed before my eyes. Like that earth movement that had obliterated the existing landscape and presented a whole new scene, I couldn't go back to my familiar surroundings. Taking a deep breath, I had slowly turned my head to face whatever lay ahead. My knees had started to tremble when my eyes collided with the teacher's hard, piercing eyes, only releasing me once she turned her gaze to the front of the class. "Class, welcome Nikki Robinson."

I heard the flat tone in the teacher's voice before turning to look at my fellow students. No one smiled. No one said a word. No one looked like me. I caught a glimpse of a few frowns and heard lots of snickering. My first day in grade 8.

In the ensuing silence, I had heard the amplified sound of my thirteen-year-old heart. The smile on my face had slipped. I pasted on a smile, pretending to be brave. The coldness in the room slammed into me, just like the change of weather a few days before, causing me to shiver.

I'm scared!

The teacher pointed to an empty seat. The one in the middle of the room. I saw the students at the front turn as I made my way to the desk. Some students looked at me then dismissed me. But I sensed eyes all around me. My face had remained frozen, and my legs felt as though they belonged to someone else. Cold sweat ran down my back, and fear slithered into my heart.

Courage, Nikki, courage.

CHAPTER THREE

Hope went up in smoke as I confronted my new life, unlike the dreams of my first day in a new school. Dreams expressed by my aunt and envied by my friends. Dreams woven on the island as I basked in the sunshine and was surrounded by friends. Dreams based on perceptions of a land where people went to fulfil their dreams.

At my previous school, everyone would clap and welcome a new student. Now faced with palpable hostility, I wanted to run and hide, to disappear.

I don't fit in; I don't belong here.

I shrank into my chair but felt the poking and the jabs. The boy across the aisle had glared at me. The one behind me poked me in the back in the middle of math class, making me wince and jerk back.

At class change time, a group of kids had surrounded me. They called me names, names I didn't know. I longed to shut off the constant insults. During recess, the girls pushed and crowded around me while the boys shouted racial slurs and egged on the girls. I turned my head when they started touching and pulling my hair.

"Urgh, feel this."

"It feels funny."

"It's so thick."

Then one of the rubber bands holding my hair in place snapped. I heard laughter; I was becoming the entertainment. Someone pushed me to the ground. I closed my eyes. The tears spilled over, and I couldn't suppress the sobs that rose in my throat. The group inched closer and closer. When they got too close, I rolled into a ball, shielding my face with my arms.

The teacher had stopped me when I returned to class. "You're filthy," she said, waiting for an explanation.

I choked. How could I explain what had happened? Would the teacher believe me? I dusted the dirt off my clothes, but my tears mingled with the dirt and stained my face. I rubbed my face, effectively smudging the stain.

The teacher's entire face had contorted with distaste before she continued. "And do something about that." She waved her hand toward my hair. "It's wild and untidy. It's distracting the other students. Make sure you keep it neat tomorrow."

My excitement had bubbled when I awoke that morning, my first day of school in my new country. I had hummed and danced, smiling to my image in the mirror as I blow-dried my hair for the first time and proudly displayed it loosely in two ponytails. After the incident at recess, my hair took on a life of its own. I removed the other rubber band and pulled most of my hair into one.

After school, I had waited until the girls' washroom was empty before tidying my hair and washing my face. The icy water helped but it couldn't wash away the pain that had settled in my chest. I leaned closer to the mirror to peer at my reflection, noticing my rumpled and messy clothes. The child with the sparkle in her eyes from the morning had disappeared, and a scared one with sad eyes stared back from the mirror. No one had warned me this could happen. Why didn't my mother or sister warn me? Did they ever experience the same thing? And if they did, why didn't they prepare me? Why? My heart wanted to go back to the comfort it knew. It desperately longed for the security the island offered. My head told me otherwise. In just one day at my new school, I had become a social pariah. Why wasn't I enough? Loneliness made an appearance, reminding me of our close relationship when everyone deserted me.

• • •

My book bag had weighed me down as I dragged my feet on the way home. It took tremendous effort to make it to the front door. I stopped to take a deep breath before stepping inside, only to come to a screeching halt.

My mother and sister stood close to the entrance. I fled into my mother's waiting arms and started to cry. We stood silently, with Val running a soothing hand along my back. After a few minutes, Marian stepped out of the embrace. "We have a lot to talk about. Let's sit."

My mother took my hands in hers. "I'm so sorry, honey. We didn't realize the first day would be so difficult for you. Please forgive me for putting you through that." She glanced at Val. "We didn't know what to expect."

She had continued after a few moments of silence. "That's why I, why we, wanted to be here when you got home. We all face racism. No matter the situation, it's always traumatic. I should have remembered that this … this is new to you." She closed her eyes and sighed deeply before taking my chin in her right hand. "You didn't grow up here, and you're so much younger than your age. I didn't intend it to be that way." She framed my face with both hands. "Sorry, honey." I waited expectantly for her to dust the unfortunate incident off her hands, sighing thankfully when she didn't. "Let me get you some hot cocoa."

Val had taken my mother's place next to me. "Sorry, Nikki. I stayed in Toronto longer than expected and didn't have time to let you know what to expect when no one in the class looks like you or speaks like you. I reminded Mama, but she must have forgotten. I let you down. I'm so sorry. It won't happen again." She gently nudged me with one shoulder. "I'm here for you. Okay?" Growing up, I had sought advice from Val rather than from my mother.

I had nodded. I appreciated their kindness, although it came too late.

The next day I followed Val's advice to pull my hair back and braid it in one, but it didn't seem to help. The verbal abuse continued. I heard it from some of the boys in my class and a group of girls in the hall.

"Your eyes are far apart."

"Your nose is too broad."

I avoided walking past more than one student for fear of taunting. When I forgot, they would gang up and utter racist slurs as they surrounded me, pulling at my book bag or pushing me around.

I had spoken once in class. Once was enough for the students to mock my island accent and intimidate me. My self-confidence had plummeted then sank even impossibly lower when I stammered for the first time in my life. "I n-n-never knew th-that." I heard snickers behind me, and I froze. When I finally finished what I was trying to say, I looked to the teacher.

"You may sit," she said.

However, it became harder and harder to hold back the tears threatening to spill over. I bit my bottom lip, praying for the bell. Then I grabbed my book bag off the floor and dashed out of the room, rubbing my face with my hands and making a beeline for the nearest girls' washroom.

At the end of that week, the teacher called me to her desk as I was about to leave class. "Nikki, please go to the principal's office."

"Miss?"

"Just go," the teacher said. "I think you're in the wrong grade."

Walking to the principal's office had filled me with dread. Did I do something wrong? Was it my hair? Sweat ran down my back, and my legs felt like Jell-O. I hesitated at the door of the principal's office.

Principal Hopkins looked up. "Come in."

When I stepped into the room, she pointed to the chair facing her desk. "Have a seat, Nikki."

I sat gingerly on the edge of the chair. "My teacher said you want to see me." I hesitated. "Something about my class."

She leaned over the large desk covered by piles of paper. "No, Nikki. It's about your grade. She thinks you're not ready for this level of work." Her voice was neutral.

I hung my head. "Oh?"

"I'm moving you to grade 7."

My stomach had knotted. I opened my mouth, but nothing came out. Afraid to speak, to ask for a reason, to question the authority. My transcripts from the island should have qualified me for grade 9, but I understood that starting in grade 8 was age appropriate in Canada. As a promising student on the island, my friends and teachers had lofty expectations that I would be successful in my chosen field.

Nothing makes sense.

Conversations with my friends about the many academic opportunities available to me in Canada seemed like a distant memory. Hopes of becoming an accountant rose like wisps of smoke dissipating into the air.

Principal Hopkins had continued. "Nikki, there's a communication problem here. Your spoken English is hard to understand. You'll need time to work on that. That's all for now. You can go," she said, returning her attention to the papers on her desk.

I had stumbled out, dazed at the unwelcomed news. Maybe they couldn't understand me, but grade 7? We spoke English in Dominica. But the principal hadn't offered support or put me in any program. How would I learn to speak so that they could understand me? Why did they hate me? Why wasn't I enough?

CHAPTER
FOUR

"The past is truly an inoperable tumour that
spreads to the present."
—Steve Toltz, *A Fraction of the Whole*

AFTER ALL THESE months, questions still haunted me. Did I expect too much? Why didn't anyone at school like me? My over-active brain kept me awake. It was impossible to say how long I thought about my first week at my school in Canada. It could have been one hour or maybe many hours. I didn't hear the front door open, so I knew my mother was still out enjoying herself somewhere. I was alone.

My siblings had moved out months after I arrived in Canada. I missed them. What would they think if I told them about the pregnancy? I needed Val's reassurance; I wanted her to know the truth, but I was too ashamed. Besides, as my mother had reminded me earlier, Val had a different life. She worked as a retail sales associate in a clothing store at one of the shopping malls in Toronto, while Keith Martin, her fiancé, enjoyed his dream job as a driver for the Toronto Transit Commission. I lived too far. I missed Val. I related to her in a way I couldn't with my mother.

It seemed that the moment I opened the box to my past, the painful memories kept rushing out, overriding all desire to sleep. With a breaking heart, I took a deep breath to relive what had happened that afternoon after the principal told me that I had to go to a lower grade.

Val had found me sobbing with my head resting on my arms at the kitchen table. "Nikki, what's wrong?"

I had shared the principal's words. "And now I have to sit with twelve-year-olds."

Val had sighed and pulled up a chair in front of me. Her hands grasped both of mine. "Listen to me, Nikki."

I looked up with puffy eyes, but the tears had stopped flowing.

"Don't tell the kids in grade 7 how old you are. They wouldn't believe you anyway," she said, casting a glance over me. "You look like a ten-year-old. Believe me, they'll just assume the school put you in a higher grade by mistake."

I lifted one shoulder to allow my jacket to catch the remnants of tears on my cheek before nodding. "Okay." I hiccupped then looked up at my sister. "Did they put you in a lower grade too?"

Val blew out air through pursed lips. "Not quite. It was slightly different for me and Eli. When we left Dominica, we went into the school system in Toronto, because that's where Mama and Daddy lived. It wasn't too bad. There were other children from the Caribbean and Africa in my school, and even a handful of Black teachers." Val paused, allowing her words to sink in.

Then she sighed heavily. "Two years ago, they also claimed that they couldn't understand us. But they kept us in the same grade. Still, they questioned our identity at every turn." Her grip tightened. "It would have been easier for you in Toronto, but when Daddy left us, we were forced to move to Kitchener. I'm sorry, Nikki. Now that I'm in the Waterloo school system, I can definitely tell you it's not as progressive as the one in Toronto. It will be challenging for you."

A look of puzzlement crossed my face.

Val shook her head and continued. "Sorry. Let me explain what I mean by challenging. It's 1981, and there aren't a lot of us in this area. We're still a novelty. So it might even take longer for the people to stop treating us like we dropped in from Mars." She smiled. "But Nikki, everything will get better with time. I promise."

I had nodded, although I was not convinced.

CHAPTER FOUR

She gently squeezed my hands. "I'll take you to Toronto tomorrow to my hairdresser to loosen your curls. Then I'll show you how to fix it so it won't stand out. Would you like that?"

"Yes," I'd said, nodding eagerly, a small smile appearing on my face. "What will she do to my hair?"

Val touched my hair. "First, she'll deep wash, detangle, and blow-dry it. Then she'll use a flat iron to straighten your hair, trim it, and style into curls."

"Can I get curls like yours?" I asked as I eyed Val's hair.

Val exuded sophistication. She looked like a model regardless of what she wore. A riot of curls framed and brought life to her face. I looked down at myself and saw someone who was the opposite—someone quiet and compliant, someone determined to please and obey. I admired Val and wanted to be like her, to revel in the opportunity to do the unexpected, to receive admiring glances from boys, to be the envy of the girls, and to be bold and fearless in dealing with my mother.

Val had laughed. "Of course."

Later, when Val had mentioned it to our mother, she tried to downplay the incident. Nevertheless, my mother had ranted and raved in her native language, calling down all sorts of evil on her ex-husband and blaming him for her situation and for ultimately causing her children pain. She calmed down after running out of steam. "Sorry, honey. I thought the education system here would have been better for you."

• • •

When we returned from getting my hair done in Toronto, Val and Eli had huddled around me as Val recounted their experiences in the city. "The first time was a revelation. Talk about culture shock!" She shook her head. "But at sixteen I gave as good as I got. Yet I still had to find ways of dealing with the constant racist comments and bullying. It wears you down. Plus, I had Eli to back me up," she said, looking at Eli and smiling. "Nobody messes with Eli."

Eli had flexed his biceps. "Nobody." He looked at me. "Just call me and I'll deal with them."

I'd grinned. People took one look and tried not to get on the wrong side of my over-six-feet, muscular brother. I lifted my hands helplessly. "Thanks, Eli. But both of you go to high school, and I'm still in junior high."

Val nodded. "Yeah. But this is a small place. It's not like in Toronto. Our schools are just a couple of blocks apart."

I sighed. "It's not only that. Everything here is new and frightening. I'm lost. I have no friends; everyone laughs when I speak, so I keep silent; they make fun of the way I look."

Eli patted my head. "You have us."

My shoulders heaved. "I know. Remember how I used to laugh a lot and sing all the time?" My siblings nodded. "Now I don't feel like singing. I wish Mama hadn't brought me here."

Val had looked at Eli and then said, "We understand, Nikki. We'll support you any way we can."

• • •

During the first school term, Val had become my main support, explaining the school system and teaching me ways to deal with my peers. Eli patted my head, but my mother had to work and couldn't attend parent–teacher meetings. With no one to advocate for me, I had to accept the dictates of the school system.

Months later, although I was hyper-visible, I had become adept at becoming invisible. I knew just when to arrive in class, didn't waste time at my locker after school, scurried down to the end of the main corridor with eyes to the ground, and hid in the girls' washroom or the library. Every. Day. The taunting had lessened but didn't stop completely. The bullies didn't get the needed response, so they ignored me for the most part. Still, the school had me questioning myself. Why wasn't I good enough?

CHAPTER
FIVE

"The past was suddenly rushing in on me
in a way I found hard to fight."
—Sebastian Faulks, *Engleby*

HUGGING THE PILLOW, I longed to find the answer to that question: Why wasn't I good enough? My stomach had twisted in knots every day as I stepped through the school doors. I had difficulty making friends there. I shut my eyes tightly, hoping to fall asleep, but the faces of fellow students swam before my eyes, mocking me, their hands reaching out, pushing me around like a football. I couldn't help but remember the first few months at my new school in Canada, or to think of how I longed to belong. I helplessly gave in to the memories.

One afternoon I had sat engrossed in a novel at the desk in the corner at the back of the library with its rows and rows of books. This was a place other students avoided. My safe space. Suddenly I felt a presence. Looking up, I had recognized the face of one of the students in my class.

Now what?

"There you are!" the student had exclaimed. I remembered her as the one who used her piercing blue eyes to effectively intimidate her fellow students.

I racked my brains but couldn't recall her name. I raised my eyes in surprise and waited.

"I looked all over for you." She looked at me without blinking.

"Oh!" Pressing into the chair, I tried unsuccessfully to disappear.

"I need to work with someone on my math," she said, looking around for a chair and moving it closer to me. "We haven't spoken before. My name is Lucy. Lucy Grant."

"Hi." My voice sounded like someone with a cold.

Lucy nodded and then stated her case. "You're much better at math than me."

"Okay," I responded, still puzzled.

Her tone held a trace of impatience. "Can you help me?"

A slow smile had appeared on my face. I relaxed.

At least she's friendly!

Lucy repeated her question. "So will you help me?"

"Sure." I nodded, giving her a genuine smile.

Our friendship had grown as we spent two afternoons every week working on math problems in the library. Lucy was strong-willed, and the negative comments from her friends hadn't prevented her from extending an occasional invitation to join her at lunch or during recess, nor did her association with me damage her popularity. When we were together, the boys smiled at her and nodded to me. Her friendship made me visible. It helped lessen the bullying. It gave me a boost of confidence.

I stood talking with Lucy outside the library one afternoon, when three guys walked past us. The one with sparkling eyes flashed her a smile. "Hey, Lucy."

"Hey."

I looked at Lucy. "Do you know him?"

"Everyone knows Brian."

"He's very … ahh … ahh … handsome." I cringed at the word *handsome*.

"Brian is a pretty boy with an empty head," Lucy said, voice sharp. "He's trouble. Forget him."

• • •

"Hey." One word. My jaw had dropped, and my eyes widened. Taking a deep breath, I inhaled and almost forgot to exhale.

"Ahh …" Then my mind went blank for a second. One word had caused me to use my hand as a fan, unzipping my jacket to let in the cool autumn breeze. A few minutes earlier, I had complained about the cold, and now I couldn't get enough of the cool air. That one word had thrown me in confusion, causing me to stop abruptly.

A smile slowly spread from ear to ear as I straightened my jacket and turned to face Lucy after one of our sessions in the library.

"Brian spoke to me! Me!" I grinned broadly. "Yeah! Yeah! Yeah!" I exclaimed, twirling around before facing my friend. "I can't believe it! Can you believe it? He remembered me from yesterday," I said in a high-pitched voice.

"Slow down, Nikki. Goodness! You're getting all excited for nothing." She snorted, gently pushing me out of her way. "He didn't speak to you. He grunted. I don't trust boys like him." She added after turning back to face me, "Don't you know the cheerleader is his girlfriend? The whole school knows it. I bet he's just being friendly."

Absentmindedly, I ran a hand over my curls, lost in another world. "Wow! I wonder if he wants to hang out with me?"

"Get real! Brian?" Lucy shook her head. "No offence, but I bet the guys here are not the same as those on the island."

I twisted my lips. "You're just jealous," I said, pulling the front of the jacket closer to my body.

Lucy's eyes changed. "Really?" Her blonde hair swayed from side to side as she shook her head in disbelief. "Make a fool of yourself. See if I care!" The glare from her eyes found its mark before she marched confidently away with her ponytail bobbing and swaying with every step.

I had muttered under my breath. "Walk away. See if I care. I don't need you." Nevertheless, my shoulders dropped at the loss of my only friend in the school. A school with so few other Black kids that the other students constantly stared and made us feel unwelcomed.

I had turned and walked in the opposite direction. Although I hated to admit it, Lucy spoke the truth. The boys on the island were different. We had done everything with innocence. The ones I knew had treated me with respect. From my limited experience, my peers on the island were babies compared to the young people I met here.

Loneliness tightened its grip on me, starving me for affection. How was I to know that every day a person from another country, from another culture, would put on a smile and step out into the world hoping for acceptance, hoping to make one friend? How was I to know that such hopes got dashed repeatedly and that the smile would fade at the end of the day?

Now that Brian, one of the most popular boys in school, had spoken one word to me, I vowed I would do anything to be seen, to be visible again. What if he was tall with mesmerizing eyes the colour of gold? What if he had deliberately tousled his hair in a practised move? Who cared? I didn't have the strength to resist the seductive whisper in my ear.

Go for it, Nikki. You have nothing to lose. You only want a friend.

CHAPTER
SIX

"It is in your moments of decision
that your destiny is shaped."
—Anthony Robbins

NOW I UNDERSTOOD what people meant when they cautioned, "Be careful what you wish for." During the first weeks at my new school, I desperately wished for a friend. Did I get my wish? I lost myself instead. Earlier in the day, the positive result had turned my world upside down. It had taken eleven months in Canada for my wish, for my actions to result in pregnancy, leaving my hopes and dreams smashed to pieces.

I barely slept that night after getting the positive result of the test. I twisted and turned, trying to remember how my actions and the decisions made for me had affected my life. When the alarm finally went off, my sheets were a tangled mess—just as my brain. I dragged myself out of bed and into the shower. But the past had a firm hold on me, and the memories flowed as fast as the water.

I groaned, lifting my face to let the water wash away the sleep but unable to wash away past thoughts of my nemesis—Brian. I hated him. Hated that when I was with him, I became desperate and mindless. In hindsight, I realized I had made a serious error in judgement when my hopeless wish for a friend caused me to ignore Lucy's warning and had driven me to make an unwise decision.

The months rolled back with the flow of the water. Over the Christmas holidays, I had lost my family support when Val announced not only her engagement but her move to Toronto to join the workforce and live with her fiancé. My mother had started working shorter hours, rushing home only to change and leave again. I did not see Eli. He busied himself with his part-time job at the local car garage or played basketball with his new friends. Once again, the road ahead had become shadowed, and I had no choice but to walk on alone.

During the second term, I had made myself available whenever Brian wanted to spend time with me. However, most of the time he simply bent over me as he leaned against the closest object to talk about himself while his two friends hovered in the background. My heart had hardened while my head had urged me to be grateful for that little show of friendship. Someone had cared enough to talk to me. Besides, I reasoned, he also helped to block not only the chilly air but also curious eyes.

I had resumed my friendship with Lucy but ignored her whenever Brian was around. Our tenuous friendship ended after an afternoon class in May. We finally had a warm day, and I looked forward to shedding my jacket to enjoy the short-lasting sun. Lucy confronted me as we stood next to our lockers in the hallway.

"Why are you still hanging around Brian?"

"What do you mean?" I kept my head straight, refusing to look at her.

"You know what I mean." Lucy looked up and down the hallway then lowered her voice. "Brian only has time for you on Tuesdays and Thursdays."

I shrugged my shoulders with indifference. "So what?"

She lost her patience. "Are you stupid or what?" She let out a long, loud groan. "Everyone knows he has a girlfriend." With hands on her hips, she continued. "His real girlfriend. The one who goes to art classes on those two nights." Every word emphasized for good measure.

I glanced briefly at Lucy. "I know." My voice came out in a low tone.

She opened her eyes wide and took a step closer. "You know? And you're still hanging around? Why?" She hissed. "What does that make you?" A brittle laugh followed. "His …"

The unmentioned next word acted like the wave of a red flag in front of a bull. I charged into Lucy, slamming her against the closest locker before she could utter the word. The students egged us on, shouting words guaranteed to increase the entertainment factor and provide food for gossip. Lucy pushed back, and the pushing and hitting continued until a teacher pulled us apart and escorted us to the principal's office.

Lucy whispered when we left the office. "I'll get you for that." We were both suspended for five days.

• • •

Excitement for the end of term could be felt throughout the school. I had started to breathe easier, counting down the days to summer vacation and a break from the drama at school. My mother remained clueless about my life, so I didn't see the point in mentioning the suspension. For five days, I pretended to go to school but sneaked off to the mall or hid in the girls' bathroom or at the back of the library. My mother put all her energy and time into dating George Plummer. She also found a new focus when Val announced her pregnancy and when Eli spent more time away from home and eventually moved out.

Therefore, the decision to accept Brian's invitation to a house party on the last Thursday before school closed had turned out to be an easy decision. I glanced out the window on the day of the party. The sun had dried up all evidence of rain from the previous night. Anticipating the warmth of the sun, I broke out into a happy dance, conducting a one-way conversation while dressing. "At least she won't be there," I said while smoothing the dress and twirling around. "My early birthday present. Happy fourteenth birthday to me! Yeah! Two months early!"

I had turned sideways to face Brian after he picked me up. "Can you turn down the music? Please."

"Why? Don't you like it?"

"It's too loud. It's hurting my ears."

"Just relax. We'll be there soon. It's only a ten-minute drive."

I curled my hands into fists and looked out the window.

The moment I stepped into the guest house of one of his friends, a wave of disappointment washed over me. Somehow I wasn't surprised to see his two shadows—Jim and Oliver. They raked me with their gaze before turning to lock eyes with their friend at my side. Then a smile passed between their faces.

Ignoring Jim and Oliver, I was more intent on taking a few steps into the room to confront Brian. "Brian, what's …"

But before I could finish speaking, Jim materialized in front of me, leaning in too close. "How about a smoke?"

"What?" I took a step back. "No. No thanks."

Jim gave a humourless laugh. "Hey. What's with the attitude? I thought all Jamaicans love that stuff."

"I'm not from Jamaica." I looked at Jim, but he had turned his back to me. "Whatever."

I can't stand that guy.

Besides, I desperately wanted to talk to Brian.

"Maybe a drink to start?" My head whipped around. I almost stumbled as I jerked back in surprise. A drink had miraculously appeared before my face. I eyed it suspiciously.

Jim's smile didn't reach his eyes. "Don't worry. It's just pop."

"Oh. Thanks."

"Enjoy." Jim gave Brian a nod before walking out with Oliver.

I whirled around to face Brian, who had yet to say a word. "Brian! What's going on? Where's the party? Where's everyone?" I looked nervously around the room.

Brian had looked at the closed door then ambled over to sit on the only couch in the room. A loveseat. His slow response gave me time to take note of my surroundings. A pool table dominated the room, but there were also a couple of games that I didn't recognize. The bar stood to the right of the door and diagonally across from a dartboard. A round table with four chairs stood by the window. Cards, empty glasses, and ashtrays filled with cigarette butts littered the surface of the table.

What place is this?

Pasting on a false smile, Brian patted the seat next to him. "Nothing. Sit. The party is here." He extended a hand to pull me closer. "Drink up."

I looked at the contents in the glass again. "Are you sure it's pop?"

"I'm sure."

"Tastes funny."

"Trust me. It's pop."

My heart had started to beat faster, and my breath came out in short bursts. The stuffiness and the cigarette odour invaded my senses, making me nauseous. When my legs grew weak and threatened to give away, I had gladly used Brian's hand to guide me to the seat. Then my muscles tightened, and I gulped down the drink to cover my unease.

Lord, help me.

The last thing I remember was seeing two images of Brian as I drained the last of my drink.

I came out of the fog and slowly opened my eyes when a faraway voice said, "Nikki. Nikki, wake up. You're home." Someone shook me.

I had swallowed with a heavy tongue, fighting to get the words out. "What?" I was unable to understand my drowsiness and disorientation.

"You're home." A second later, Brian opened the door on the passenger side and hurriedly helped me out of the car. He drove off while I stood swaying on the sidewalk.

I had lost track of time. The thought *Mama's not home* came from the deepest recesses of my mind as I staggered on the empty driveway and made it to my room with a fuzzy mind.

• • •

Over the summer holidays, I had joined a team of students who helped clean the church on Mondays after Sunday service and fellowship, and on Thursdays after mid-week activities. Mrs. Carmen and the other members of the church threw a surprise baby shower for Val at the end of July. The party was well attended. I soaked it all in as I observed how everyone gave Val wonderful baby gifts and fussed around the mother-to-be. They asked about baby names, about the baby's gender, about the wedding. Val explained that they planned to have the wedding after the baby was born. The celebration brought back happy island memories for me.

In August, I realized that I had missed my period, but I shrugged it off, assuming it was late. However, I found myself dozing off during the day and craving sweets, especially ice cream, more than normal. Then a wave of nausea swept over me. Something had clicked and fallen into place. The thought hit hard, like a punch to my stomach. I doubled over moaning.

"No. No. No. This can't be happening." I sank to the floor groaning. "What do I do?"

The next morning, I knew I had to get a pregnancy test. Fast. I had staked out the neighbourhood drugstore and snuck in after a young Black girl left. I grabbed a rapid pregnancy test, slamming the money on the counter. My voice came out breathless. "Sorry, my sister forgot to pick this up." I ran out of the store before the cashier could give me the change.

In the confines of my bathroom, I fumbled with the box, anxiously skimming the instructions, but then I had to reread the leaflet a few times before understanding what to do. My mind became numb and chills wracked my body as I sat on the bathroom floor waiting for the results. I glanced at the clock. Luckily, I had the day off from my summer job at the church. It would be hours before my mother got home.

• • •

I turned off the shower. Was that only yesterday? It seemed a lifetime ago. Another lifetime. My sigh came out deep, full of regret, shame, and uncertainty. Time to figure out what to wear, since the morning brought more of the same hot and humid weather with a chance of an isolated thunderstorm in the evening. The heat warning continued with the advice to stay indoors. I gladly welcomed the advisory, since it gave me an opportunity to get away from the watchful eyes of my mother and to spend time with my siblings at the Caribbean Bistro in Kitchener, usually referred to as the Bistro.

I finally settled on a bright yellow sundress and added a couple of beaded bracelets to complete my look. Everyone would assume that I chose them for the weather, but the fact remained that I needed to boost my confidence and deflect scrutiny from my family.

Five minutes later, my mother called. "Nikki, time to go."

"Coming," I said, taking a last look in the mirror. Was I strong enough to tell my siblings, or would I continue to keep my situation a secret?

Lord, help me.

CHAPTER
SEVEN

"Unfortunately, the clock is ticking, the hours are going
by. The past increases, the future recedes. Possibilities
decreasing, regrets mounting."
—Haruki Murakami, *Dance Dance Dance*

I GOT OUT of the car, following along slowly after some hesitation, to see my mother preening in front of the top glass on the entrance door of the restaurant. Taking a small step back, I waited patiently, a reluctant witness as my mother used the glass as a mirror. She checked her lipstick, tilted her head, turned it from one side to the next before running her hands over her black and white polka dot dress, and dusted imaginary lint off the white jacket with padded shoulders. She gave a satisfied smile before opening the door and stepping into the air-conditioned restaurant.

The Bistro occupied two regular storefronts along the main street in downtown Kitchener. The simple interior displayed framed island scenes on its walls, and a few well-placed palms sat in the corners. Piped-in reggae and jazz music completed the ambience. My mother gazed around. "This is nice. Did I mention that George recommended the brunch? The Bistro only offers it on Saturdays."

The host guided us to a smaller room on the side of the main dining room, informing us that they sometimes reserved it for parties and special guests. She explained that the brunch menu consisted of ackee and saltfish, crab cakes, jerk chicken, waffles with mango syrup, and a brunch platter, leaving us with a few menus while we waited for the rest of our party.

My mother scanned the menu before making small conversation. "I like their lunch and dinner menu." The restaurant served homestyle Caribbean dishes such as jerk chicken, oxtail stew, seafood-based meals, curry, and roti with vegetarian options. Marian looked toward the entrance of the room then bounced up. A smile broke on her face and her voice became animated. "My favourite person!"

I looked up from the menu and saw George Plummer standing there. I kept my gaze on my mother, half expecting her to float toward him, before silently sucking my teeth.

When George sauntered in, I noticed his checkered shirt and pants, then his white calf socks and boat shoes that, in my opinion, fell far short of a fashion statement. Nevertheless, his eyes lit up when he caught a glimpse of my mother. Pausing briefly to smooth the few wayward hairs on his balding head, he quickened his steps, making a beeline for her. After reaching up to hug her, he turned sideways but didn't make eye contact with me. "Oh! Happy birthday." Then he ignored me and engaged my mother in a private conversation. She basked under George's adoration, blind to his slight of me.

Talk about crashing a party empty-handed.

Five minutes later, my larger-than-life brother, Eli, dressed in khaki pants, a brightly coloured polo shirt, and penny loafers, entered with his girlfriend, Donna Fraser. Growing up, my older brother, with his big personality and big laugh, had regularly irritated me by patting my head and calling me Shrimp. I had gotten even by calling him High Boy.

Donna's wide smile lit up her hazel eyes, and her curly brown hair, in a side ponytail, blended with her brightly coloured jumpsuit. Donna acknowledged the others before bending to wrap me in a sweet birthday hug. Their presence brought life and energy to the room.

Eli hugged me and put a gift bag on a side table. Although nicknames had remained in the past, he couldn't resist the familiar pat on my head. I beamed at him. After greeting our mother and George, he promptly scanned the menu then turned to Donna. "Wow! Look at the spread! It's going to be hard to decide what to eat. Everything looks amazing." Without pausing, he called. "Hey, George, what do you recommend?"

CHAPTER SEVEN

George reluctantly took his eyes off my mother. "It's all good, man. I've tried almost every dish." His Jamaican accent was still pronounced after ten years in Canada. He added as an afterthought, "You know the owner."

Eli lifted his eyebrows. "I do? Who?"

"Mrs. Carmen."

"Oh, yeah! I've tasted her food at church. The woman can cook!" Before Eli could select, Val and her fiancé, Keith Martin, appeared at the entrance.

Val, glowing with her pregnancy, entered ahead of Keith. She wore a loose-flowing dress that enhanced her growing baby bump. Although Val towered over me by about four inches, we came by our complexion and hair texture naturally from our father, while Eli favoured our mother. Keith, dressed in a pair of blue jeans, added the gift bags to the side table and adjusted his button-down shirt.

Is this what I'll look like in a few months?

They greeted everyone before finding their places at the table. However, in the blink of an eye, Marian stood over Val, fussing like a mother hen. Val caught my eyes as she settled into the chair next to me. She whispered, "Sorry, Nikki."

I shrugged, appearing unconcerned, but my heart broke. "It's okay."

Val asked, "Do you want to open your gifts now?"

Eli answered for me. "I'm starving! Nikki, can you wait until we finish the main course? Just before dessert?"

I grinned. "Sure, Eli."

After everyone ordered, Val turned to me and whispered, "What did Mama give you?"

I avoided answering the question. "Isn't she paying for brunch?"

"Not quite. Eli and I are also sharing the cost."

I remained speechless as Val leaned in to touch me. "We've got your back. I like how you've done your hair. I remember how you used to love your hair braided in two. Makes you look younger and innocent."

My sister's honest words were like arrows stabbing at my heart. The pain took me by surprise, causing me to bend forward and place a hand to my chest.

"Are you okay?" Val's voice held concern.

"Yes. Just the excitement."

I shifted my weight from side to side, allowing my gaze to rest on everyone sitting around the table. Their excited voices made me dislike this new me. I loved the people gathered to celebrate another year of my life, but the sweet, naïve child they knew and loved had turned into a failure. What had I done?

It was just a party with Brian—a boy I hardly knew.

My thoughts wandered throughout the meal. If they knew my secret, they'd be ashamed of me. My hopes washed up on the shore and just as quickly disappeared as the waves retreated into the ocean. One foolish mistake.

This celebration was different than my last birthday in Dominica, when my life was carefree, when going to the beach and eating an ice cream cone with my friends brought me joy and happiness. This year, it was as if the rivers had flooded their banks and washed away everything after the storm.

I looked up when the server placed my order on the table. The waffles came with a side order of fruits, chopped nuts, melted butter, and a small jug of mango syrup. I watched mesmerized as the melted butter fell and slowly pooled into every dimpled corner of the waffles.

Why couldn't I settle and find my place like the melted butter? I found myself facing a serious dilemma. My mind refused to think of anything else.

How did I manage to create this maelstrom?

I became totally absorbed with the flow of the butter. Unable to look away, unable to protest. My sister's laugh brought me back to the present moment. I blinked, becoming aware of my surroundings. Plastering a smile on my face, I looked around. Had they even noticed? I poured syrup over my waffles and added a handful of chopped nuts. As I bit into the crisp crunch of the waffle, I was unaware of the powdered sugar falling on my dress. I closed my eyes to savour the sweet mango taste, but it unwittingly prevented me from staying in the present, causing the syrup to lose its flavour and leave a sour taste in my mouth.

I wiped my mouth with the napkin but couldn't erase the past. I braced myself. The storm was just getting started.

CHAPTER
EIGHT

"Memories are dangerous things. You turn them over
and over, until you know every touch and corner, but still
you'll find an edge to cut you."
—Mark Lawrence, *Prince of Thorns*

ELI CALLED MY name. "Wow! That waffle put you in a deep trance. I called your name a couple of times. It must be delicious. Can I taste it?" Everyone laughed good-humouredly.

"Sure," I said, honouring his request. I admired that about Eli. He knew what he wanted. As a minor, I still depended on my mother for direction. She was in deep conversation with George. I felt a distance between myself and my mother. Why was that?

The memories flew faster and faster, and I couldn't keep up with them. They were like powerful hurricane winds I had to live through until they ended.

I had a vague recollection that years earlier, when I lived on the island, my father's family disliked my mother. I had found out that bit of information on the day I had snuck into the kitchen to get a cookie from the cookie jar and inadvertently overheard a conversation in which they called my mother selfish and greedy, putting her interest before that of her family. Did that knowledge cause me to keep her at a distance? Or was that the way it had always been? Was that why I think of her as Marian or my mother, never as Mama, unless in conversation?

Yet I also remembered when my mother had stepped up weeks after I started school in Canada to find a place where I belonged and where I could be part of a community. A few days before Thanksgiving, my mother had informed us that she was going to spend the following Sunday with us.

Val had leaned against the door frame in the living room and smiled. "That's nice. You're getting the day off."

Marian had nodded. "Yes." She paused. "It's time we go back to church."

Surprised, we had stared at her. Val straightened, but her voice came out a pitch higher than normal. "Go back to church? Where? What church? Did you find one?" We belonged to one of the traditional churches, but Marian hadn't tried to find one after moving to the area.

Eli grumbled. "Wait. Aren't we going to talk about the menu for Thanksgiving dinner?" He walked further into the room and sucked his teeth, looking disinterested.

Marian had ignored his outburst. "We'll have a Thanksgiving meal, but first we're going to attend one of the Black churches in the area."

Val had stiffened. "Why?" She spent weekends in Toronto.

Our mother had sat down and waved us to do the same. "My friend told me about some churches in the area that are becoming gathering places for the Black community. And believe me, we desperately need our community." She paused to look at us. "There's something else. It's also one way all of you, and especially you, Nikki, can meet other Black kids."

Val had relaxed. "Can you tell us more? How will it help Nikki?"

Our mother had nodded. "Sure. We're going to a church here in Kitchener. It provides different social activities."

"That sounds interesting," added Eli. "It will be good for all of us." He looked at me. "And Nikki, you'll meet kids your own age. It will be good for you. You'll have fun."

Our mother nodded. "Then it's settled."

Both Val and Eli had smiled at me before Eli said, "Anything for Nikki."

Marian added for good measure, "And it will allow us to strengthen our faith at the same time." She didn't expect a response.

• • •

CHAPTER EIGHT

On Thanksgiving Sunday, we had attended the worship service at a church close to us. Mrs. Carmen had introduced us to the other members, who welcomed us. Mrs. Carmen's kindness and empathy putting me at ease.

I had an instant connection with Mrs. Carmen. She reminded me of an island aunty—someone not related to you but one who garnered your love. Her soft and gentle voice reassured and invited confidence at the same time. Mrs. Carmen appeared to be the same age as my mother, and standing next to Marian, she stood tall, although she lifted her chin to hold a conversation with my mother.

I had whispered to Val, "I thought Mrs. Carmen was married. Where's her husband? Did we meet him?"

"Someone mentioned he died."

"Oh! That's sad. But she doesn't look sad."

"Maybe he died a long time ago. Come on. Let's talk to her."

• • •

Marian had looked over her shoulder at us as she drove home afterwards. "I hope everyone enjoyed the first visit. What do you think?"

"Lots of kids in Nikki's age group, so that's good," Eli said. "However, I noticed the basketball hoop as soon as we drove in, even before we parked. That's what I call welcoming! I've already hooked up with a few of the guys." He laughed dryly. "They indicated the court was the best place to take out your anger and frustrations. I need a place like that."

My mother had glanced at Eli in the rear-view mirror. "I knew that would interest you. What about you, Valerie?"

Val had shrugged her shoulders, staring straight ahead. "It's okay. I like the sense of community. Something that could work for Nikki. But you know I like to spend my weekends in Toronto," she continued hurriedly, not giving Marian an opportunity to object. "Anyway, I noticed a few interesting activities. I'll go with Nikki to the mid-week ones."

Marian ignored Val's comment about Toronto. "Nikki?"

I glanced at my mother from the back seat. "I like it. It reminds me of the community we had on the island. It's not too far. I can even take the bus by myself."

Marian had smiled. "I agree. Everyone, especially Mrs. Carmen, was extremely helpful and welcoming. She seemed to connect with you, Nikki. I noticed you were in a deep conversation with her." She paused briefly. "Now I don't have to worry about you," she said, returning to the perfect world in her head.

CHAPTER
NINE

"A mountain is composed of tiny grains of earth. The
ocean is made up of tiny drops of water. Even so, life is
but an endless series of little details, actions, speeches,
and thoughts. And the consequences whether good or
bad of even the least of them are far-reaching."
—Swami Sivananda

LOUD LAUGHTER PULLED me away from painful memories and back to the
people around the table. I passed another waffle and the mango syrup to Eli
but toyed with what remained on my plate. I smiled looking at Eli enjoying his
meal, then between Eli and Val. Their support had remained constant and
their love unquestionable. But they couldn't protect me all the time. My confidence deserted me, even now at the restaurant with my family around me.
Marian and George were in a world of their own. Donna and Eli expressed
their delights in the taste of the food while Val and Keith shared a compan-
ionable meal. But sitting next to Val, I felt like a child.

The smell of fried plantain and crab cakes brought back memories of
comfort and belonging, but instead of gladdening my heart, it tightened the
cloak of loneliness around me.

Val touched my arm. "Hey! You didn't eat much." I glanced at my plate
with a half-eaten waffle, my appetite deserting me during the passing of my
mental storm.

"Are you okay?"

I nodded.

"Ready to open your gifts?"

Eli gallantly placed the two gift bags on the table before me. Val and Keith's gift included a bomber jacket, pyjamas, and a robe. I received a couple of pairs of socks and a pair of jeans from Eli and Donna, along with a few tops.

Val whispered, "I didn't see a bag from George. Did he give you anything?"

I shook my head and thanked everyone. Eli must have guessed at Val's question because they both turned to look at George. However, before they could utter a word, my mother held up a gift bag. "One more gift!" Val looked at me, but I shrugged my shoulders.

Marian gazed at our faces. "It's for the baby."

My heart jolted.

Val exclaimed, "Mama, we just had a baby shower. Please, no more gifts. Let's wait until the baby is born."

Marian grinned. "I know. I couldn't resist this adorable blanket. It's a grandmother's prerogative."

Val groaned. "Okay, Mama. Thank you." She closed her eyes briefly and sighed before turning to our brother. "Ready for dessert, Eli?"

Eli rubbed his palms together. "Bring it on."

Mrs. Carmen brought the dessert cart. "Happy birthday, Nikki. I wanted to do this personally." She looked at the faces around the table. "Dessert is on the house. Enjoy." Smiling, she looked at me. "I'll see you at church."

• • •

Church became my haven after the brunch. My safe harbour. I hung around the church every day, although I was only assigned to clean on Mondays and Thursdays. I didn't want to think about my situation. However, shame and guilt prevented me from enjoying the activities. I avoided everyone. I kept my head bent and no one approached me whenever I busied myself with work.

Mrs. Carmen stopped me one day. "Nikki, dear, are you okay?"

I nodded. "Yes, ma'am," finding it difficult to muster a smile.

Mrs. Carmen looked at me intently but didn't press the issue. She sighed. "Okay, dear. I'm here if you need me."

CHAPTER NINE

"Thank you, Mrs. Carmen," I said, hoping she wouldn't see the pain in my eyes. My eyes remained downcast, and I worked twice as hard as everyone else, sometimes cleaning areas already cleaned. Everyone smiled. "Such a diligent worker!" However, I noticed Mrs. Carmen keeping a watchful eye on me.

• • •

Although the days dragged, I didn't have time to process my dilemma before the new school year arrived. I had once considered my jeans snug-fitting, but now tears ran unchecked down my face as I twisted and turned in the struggle to wriggle into them. Using the bed for support made the task easier, but it made me realize that in a few months I'd have to resort to wearing loose clothes.

I stumbled out of my room and headed for the front door, but my mother's voice reached me before I could escape. "Aren't you going to eat something?"

What's she doing home?

I didn't turn around. "No. I'll be late for school."

• • •

My isolation worsened when I started grade 8. The students ignored me, Lucy was no longer my friend, and I avoided Brian. I had no one. To make matters worse, I couldn't shake Lucy's constant vigilance. I caught her staring at me every time I lifted my head in class. I saw her watching me in the hallways, before and after school. Always watching from a distance. Lucy seemed to monitor my every move for five days.

The stress became too much for me. I had no time for subterfuge the afternoon I threw up in the girls' bathroom. I had prepared a plausible explanation in case anyone heard me. Sagging against the sink, I held a hand over my chest after realizing I was alone in the bathroom. I leaned closer to the mirror. Who was this girl with haunted eyes? Taking a deep breath, I walked out with a confident stride only to come to an abrupt stop. I gave an involuntary gasp, preferring a douse from a bucket of icy water to confronting Lucy Grant.

Her book bag hung over one shoulder while she leaned the other shoulder against the wall facing the washroom entrance. I had tossed and turned during the nights, wondering how and when Lucy would retaliate for getting suspended for five days after our fight toward the end of the last school year. The shock left me incapable of movement.

My heart rate increased rapidly, and I had difficulty breathing. My palms grew damp, and small droplets of sweat began to form on my forehead as I stared into Lucy's cold eyes and saw her triumphant smile. She looked me straight in the eye. Her smile grew sinister as she held my gaze. I watched helplessly as Lucy straightened, adjusted her bag, and walked away. My legs buckled. I sagged against the closest wall, let out a deep breath, and wiped my forehead.

Courage, Nikki, courage.

Sleep eluded me that night. It had turned cold overnight, and I longed to stay in bed and hide under the covers. But my fate awaited me. After I arrived at school, Principal Hopkins summoned me to her office. I gathered my books slowly before casting a side glance at Lucy. She stared at me with hard eyes and a victorious smile before looking away, thus confirming my worst fears.

The walk to the office seemed longer than usual. My upset stomach and throbbing headache grew with every slow and agonizing step taking me to a certain end, casting me in the role of a dead woman walking. Principal Hopkins didn't offer me a seat. She didn't waste time on pleasantries. "Is it true you're pregnant?"

I opened my mouth. Nothing came out. I couldn't speak.

My silence annoyed the principal, who shook her head.

"Nikki, you know this is unacceptable. I have no option but to expel you."

My body flashed hot, icy cold, then hot. I broke out in a sweat. With a heavy heart, I bowed my head, dragging my dishonour, humiliation, and shame as I crawled out of the office. Once in the hallway, my body started to shake. My face twitched as I fought against tears.

I had the entire day to figure out how to break the news to my mother.

The storm had reached maximum storminess.

CHAPTER
TEN

"I believe we are solely responsible for our choices, and
we have to accept the consequences of every deed,
word, and thought throughout our lifetime."
—Elizabeth Kubler-Ross

I SAT DRY-EYED like a robot at the kitchen table, planning and discarding every excuse and disclosure. Darkness closed in. The decision of where to lay the blame seem to swell until it loomed ominously at the forefront of my mind. I knew where my mother would lay the blame. But didn't some of the blame lie with her? The tears moved closer to the surface as Marian's arrival time drew near. I hoped that the rain that had started early in the afternoon and was continuing into the night would delay her arrival.

The front door banged, signalling that my mother was home. She turned on the lights in the kitchen, squeaked, and almost dropped the grocery bag in her hand. "Goodness, child. You almost gave me a heart attack. For crying out loud! Why are you sitting in the dark?"

Waiting for an answer, Marian rested the bag on the table and grabbed a few paper towels to wipe her hands and remnants of the rain off the bag. She looked at me sharply when I didn't respond. "You're crying. Are you hurt? What's the matter? Why are you crying?"

My breath grew faster, and fresh tears ran down my face. "I'm sorry, Mama." I didn't attempt to wipe them away.

Marian stopped wiping away the water and stood still before giving me her full attention. "Sorry? Why are you sorry?"

My heart raced. I looked at the floor, hoping that it would rise up and swallow me. "I got expelled," my voice barely a whisper.

The paper towel dropped unnoticed to the floor. Marian pulled the closest chair and dropped heavily into it. "What! Expelled? Why?"

I choked. "Ahh ... umm ..." I was hoping to delay saying the word.

My mother leaned closer. "Speak up, child. Why? Why were you expelled?" Her voice grew sharp, commanding obedience.

"I ... I'm pregnant," I said, starting to tremble.

My mother shot out of the chair. "You're what?"

"I'm ..." I tried to make myself disappear into the chair.

My mother raised a hand with the palm facing toward me. "I heard you. I heard you the first time. I just can't believe it." She took a deep breath. "I didn't even know you had a boyfriend. Who is the father?"

Although my heart rate increased, I tried to stall, casting my eyes downward and shuffling my feet.

"Answer me. Who is he?" she asked with a snap.

I closed my eyes and clenched my jaw.

"Lord, help me." She looked upward. "Child, you're underage." She beat her chest. "Do you know what that means?" she asked, not wanting or waiting for me to answer. "I'll tell you what it means. I don't know about this country, but as far as I know, it's illegal. It's a criminal act. It's statutory rape."

I knew she would say that.

I raised my head but didn't look her in the eye when I lied. "It wasn't rape." Did I make the right decision? How would the lie affect my future?

My mother glared at me. "I don't care what you say. You're underage. It can only be rape."

I bit my bottom lip to keep it from quivering. "I agreed." My voice came out in a whisper and I wished I were anywhere but here.

Marian raised her voice. "You agreed? Why? I know you, Nikki Robinson, and I know when you're lying. This isn't you. Why? Why did you do something so stupid? I thought you were smarter than that."

"I wanted him to be my friend." My heart hurt and my throat ached with the effort it took to hold back my tears. There were hundreds of butterflies in my stomach. I bowed my head under the heavy load.

"Who is he? Tell me. Why do you want to protect someone who doesn't deserve to be protected?"

My head remained bowed. Waiting. Waiting for her biting words.

Marian paced on the spot. "What happened? Are you ashamed? I certainly hope so. Do you know the amount of shame this will bring on this family? I didn't have that problem with Valerie. No, sir! Everyone said you were the good girl. Didn't you listen to anything we taught you? How could you? I blame your father. He spoiled you too much. His princess indeed! Look at you now. Pregnant."

With that word, Marian slumped into the chair, put her hands over her head, and started to wail. "Lord, have mercy! Bon Dieu, bon Dieu! Chile, what have you done? You're only fourteen. Did I bring you here to get pregnant?"

She stared at me but didn't expect an answer. "How can I hold my head up high in church? People will think I'm not a good mother. They'll say I have no control over my chile." The wailing resumed. After a few minutes, a thought suddenly occurred to her. She asked hopefully, "Wait. Are you sure? Did you see a doctor?"

I shook my head, still afraid of making eye contact. My face crumpled as tears spilled over and ran down my cheeks.

Marian's sigh came from a mother's pain. "Then that's the first thing we'll do. I also need time to figure out how to deal with this. This situation." She waved her hand in the air and then continued wailing and crying.

• • •

I was grateful that my mother had to work and couldn't accompany me to the doctor's office. While I waited, my eyes wandered over the display pamphlets, zeroing in on those about social issues. I looked around the empty office before hastily selecting the one dealing with sexual violence and stuffed it in my purse.

After the doctor finished his examination, he looked into my eyes. "How old are you, Nikki?" His eyes were kind.

"Fourteen."

"You know that means you're underage."

I hung my head. "Yes. I'm sorry."

"I'm sorry too, Nikki. What can you tell me about the father?"

"I … ahhh … why?" My heart raced.

He sighed heavily. "You're only fourteen, Nikki. I must file a report."

All sorts of complications flashed before my eyes. "Oh! Even if I agreed?"

"Did you?"

I gulped. "Yes. Yes, Doctor."

He raised his eyebrows before handing me a pamphlet from his desk. "I'd like you to read this. It will give you information on resources if you need them. Or you can return if anything changes."

"Thank you," I said, adding it to the one in my purse. "Are you still going to file a report?"

"Not if you say it's consensual."

My heart rate slowed. "Oh, okay."

"Please ask your mother to phone for the results."

"My mother?"

"Yes."

• • •

A couple of days later, my mother paced back and forth in front of the television set, groaning in despair every time she glanced at me. Finally, she stopped to face me. "So it's confirmed. You're pregnant."

She stopped pacing. "You know, the doctor wanted to know if I wished to report your pregnancy. He told me it was my responsibility and obligation to do so. But when I told him it was consensual, he was kind enough to tell me the legal ramifications if it were otherwise."

"Oh." I didn't have to ask. I knew my mother couldn't resist telling me what she'd learned.

"It was a lot. First, he'd have to file a report, then the police and social worker would get involved. Do you know they could take you away? Away from this home"—she snapped her fingers—"just like that. But for me, the best part would be that the boy's name would appear on the Sex Offenders Register. He would pay for what he did." She glared at me. "Now none of that will happen." Raising a finger, she proclaimed, "But heaven help the boy if I ever find out his name."

I mumbled something unintelligible.

She ignored me for a few minutes. When she lifted her head, her voice sounded like doom. "But let's get one thing straight, missy. You're not having an abortion." My mother continued in her preaching voice. "I wouldn't allow it. I believe it's immoral to take a life. A life you don't have the God-given right to terminate."

My mother pressed her lips together in a thin line of determination, but her eyes showed disapproval. "You must place the baby up for adoption. It's for your own good. What can you give this child?"

I bowed my head to observe each tear slipping off my face, forming a mini puddle on the floor.

Love. I could give love.

"You know people will call the child all sorts of bad names. Besides, no man will marry you if they know you have a child."

I looked up but didn't have the energy or the will to contradict her. Anything I said would be pointless. It would be begging for trouble.

"I'm only protecting you. You're so young. You have so much ahead of you. Like college. One day you'll marry and have children."

I moved restlessly in the chair, causing my mother to narrow her eyes and ask in a matter-of-fact voice, "Nikki? What did you tell Valerie and Eli?

"Nothing." My heart hurt. I wanted to tell Val, but shame kept me quiet.

"Good. I'll tell them. It will be better coming from me. Besides, Eli would go crazy and do something idiotic in an attempt to find the truth, and Valerie is no better. She'd have a silly idea like suggesting you live with her. I can't have any of that."

I looked at my feet, certain my mother would paint me in a bad light. I had no control over the situation.

My mother sat down. "We can't let people know." After a few minutes, she continued. "This is what I'm going to do. If anyone at the church asks, I'll tell them you're finding it hard to adjust to life in Canada. You were acting up. I had to send you to live with your cousin in Toronto. Mrs. Carmen would be so disappointed in you if she knew the truth." She glanced at my flat stomach. "Sorry, Nikki, but it's best if you go somewhere where no one knows you."

Banished.

I took a deep breath and bowed my head as tears escaped through my closed eyes.

• • •

My mother looked over her shoulder while putting away the groceries after her weekly shopping. "I tried to get you into the home for pregnant teens in Cambridge, but they had no space. However, I found a place where you can stay. It's a place for troubled teenage girls." She paused briefly. "Seems you qualify. You're an unwed mother. I had to plead your case, but in the end, they agreed to take you."

I interrupted with a hopeful voice. "Is it in Toronto? Can I see Val?"

Marian shook her head. "No. It's not in Toronto. It's a couple of towns over. And no, you can't see Valerie. That's not a good idea. Knowing that you're pregnant would only upset her. I don't want her upset. You know she's going to have her baby soon. It's not good to give her any undue stress."

"Oh."

Her voice softened at the crestfallen look on my face. "Maybe you can see her in a few months. The place indicated that you have the option to stay there on weekends and holidays or you can come home. Something to think about."

I nodded.

She took a breath. "Let's not get off track. We were talking about the place I found for you, about La Bonne Maison. Apparently, everyone calls it La Maison. They're willing to take you next week. Isn't that great? Although I spoke with them, they'll also explain everything to you, including options to visit home. We agreed that you'll stay there until you have the baby. The best part is that they'll even make plans for the adoption. You won't have to worry about that."

Like washing my hands.

She looked back at me. "Ahh, I told them the baby is biracial. I hope I didn't tell a lie."

No.

I shook my head, but my eyes glazed over at her assumption. I lost my voice again. Why didn't they tell me that moving to Canada would be like walking through a minefield?

CHAPTER
ELEVEN

"Grief can be a burden, but also an anchor. You get used
to the weight, how it holds you in place."
—Sarah Dessen, *The Truth about Forever*

I STEPPED OUT of the car, taking a good look at La Maison. It was an ordinary building surrounded by flowers and shrubs, looking just like the other family homes in the area. However, the inviting façade did nothing to change my view of it as a prison.

My mother parked the car and exited. After taking a few steps toward the entrance, she stopped to look over her shoulder. "Is something wrong?"

"No."

"Then stop dilly-dallying. I have papers to sign. Let's go in." I heard her suck her teeth.

I looked around while the administrator, Susan Knight, handed Marian a few papers to sign. Then my mother bent and pecked me on the cheek, saying, "Bye, Nikki," before hurrying out of the room.

The pain of rejection and loneliness I experienced when I was left behind on the island, when I had waved goodbye to Val and Eli, returned tenfold. Abandoned and parentless. I gritted my teeth and blinked as fast as I could, but I couldn't prevent the tears from rising. I turned my eyes upward, trying unsuccessfully to stop the moisture from spilling over. I helplessly wiped my eyes and cheeks with my sleeves, trying to remove the tear stains and get myself under control before looking at Susan.

She gave me a sympathetic smile and explained that the home was a government-run facility, and I was the youngest and only pregnant teen in La Maison. "Since it's publicly funded, all residents are required to work. We also encourage interested residents to use gardening as a form of therapy. We have one or two who love to plant flowers and vegetables in the spring. But it's all voluntary."

"Okay." Taking a deep breath, I asked. "Where will I work?"

She looked at me with a slight smile. "In a restaurant. Because you are so young, I could only get you assigned to washing dishes and cleaning. However, you can help the La Maison workers when you're no longer able to perform your duties at the restaurant."

I sat up straight when Susan continued. "I've contacted the Children's Aid Society, and they'll assign you a case worker. You'll meet her tomorrow. You have the rest of the day to settle in and meet the other residents. You'll start working the day after tomorrow."

"Okay."

She continued, "You'll meet everyone in time. Besides the cook and housekeeper, we have a residential supervisor, and one staff member who is always present during the day." She stood up. "Come, let me show you around and take you to your room."

The administrator's office occupied a space on the main floor, and the residents met with the case worker in the meeting room next door. The communal areas, including a powder room, the supervisor's quarters, and the kitchen, occupied the rest of that floor. The basement was reserved for laundry, storage, and utility. The four bedrooms occupied the top floor, and the residents shared the single bathroom.

My room held a twin bed with a night table to the right and underneath the window. I noticed a comfortable armchair on the other side of the window, and a chest of drawers, desk, and chair were neatly tucked into the rest of the compact space.

• • •

I pretended to be watching television when the other residents returned from work. I felt like a fish out of water, unsure of what to say to the other residents, unsure of myself. But one of them, Anna Landry, came over to sit next to me. The smile in Anna's eyes welcomed me, not caring that I was the only Black face in La Maison.

Anna was slender and of medium height with deep, mysterious eyes and brunette hair pulled back in a ponytail that reached past her shoulders. I warmed up to the older teenager, who reminded me of Lucy Grant. I'd made the mistake of dismissing Lucy and not valuing her friendship. I had learned my lesson and knew how important it was to find support and friendship with another resident.

"There's nothing much on the television," Anna leaned over to whisper to me. "Are you okay with us sitting on the couch over there?" She turned her gaze toward the back of the room.

I nodded.

When we were seated, Anna smiled. "Did anyone tell you why this place is called La Bonne Maison?"

I shook my head.

She leaned forward, speaking in a dramatic voice. "The founders were from Quebec. Seems their only child, a girl, ran away from home at sixteen. During the winter. And just before a terrible snowstorm. They didn't find her body until a winter thaw. Her parents wanted other teenage girls to have a safe harbour when in trouble, and a place to stay as long as they wanted."

I put a hand to my lips and whispered. "Oh!"

Anna leaned back with a satisfied smile and a gleam in her eyes. "Yes, I know. Gets me every time."

After a few uncomfortable minutes, Anna cleared her throat. "This must be hard for you." She paused when I looked sharply at her, putting up her hands in a defensive position. "It's okay. You're not alone. Everyone here has problems. Although we're years older, we all have assigned case workers."

I bowed my head, regretting my suspicion.

Anna sighed. "They've labelled us troubled teens. We're here because we can't live at home. I came here two years ago when I was seventeen. I grew up in a religious but dysfunctional family." She went on to explain what caused her to leave home and seek shelter at La Maison.

In the end she gave a dry laugh. "We tend to give one another space, but come to me if you need anything. Anything at all. I usually know what's going on, so let me know if you have any questions." She added as an after-thought. "You know … you're lucky."

Luck was not a word with which I had a close association, but I couldn't help asking, "I am?"

"Like I said, I've been here for about two years. We were at full capacity for over a year. I know there's a waiting list because I was on it for about six months. Then unexpectedly one of the residents decided it was time to move back home. Just in time for you to move in," she said, looking thoughtful. "Someone is praying for you. Always remember that. Remember that when you're at your lowest and darkness is creeping in. Remember that when you think your cross is too heavy to bear." She stood and rested a hand on my shoulder. "Welcome to La Maison."

• • •

The following day the case worker, Tammy Davis, discussed the pros and cons of keeping the baby. Tammy was in her late twenties with a bubbly personality and an optimistic view of life. But everything about the adoption process confused me. I summoned a bit of courage to engage Tammy in discussion, since she treated me as an adult and exercised patience. "I thought the baby went to the new parents right away. I don't understand."

"First of all, you have six months to change your mind," Tammy said patiently.

"Do you mean I can sign the papers and then take the baby back before the end of six months?"

"Yes. It does happen."

"Why would the mother change her mind?"

"There are several reasons. The mother might think she made a mistake, her family finally agreed to help her raise the baby, or the baby's father changed his mind. In this case, it's a mother's prerogative to change her mind."

"I see. Sorry to ask all these questions. So when do the new parents get to adopt the child?"

Tammy answered after a brief pause. "Unfortunately, we have situations where the court can sometimes tie up a child for a long time. Every case is different."

"Then what happens to the baby in the meantime?"

"The baby goes to foster care."

"Foster care? Why?"

"There's a reason for that. You see, the prospective parents are required to go through parent training."

I touched my stomach. "So we have no control. Our babies also suffer!"

Tammy sympathized with me. "The sad part is that you don't get to bond with your child, and neither does the new family."

Tears rolled down my cheeks.

Tammy gently touched my arm. "We'll continue this discussion another day."

I nodded, wiping away the tears.

She added, "One more thing you should know."

My heart sank. "What?" Could anything be worse?

"I don't mean to make matters worse, but I must let you know biracial children are harder to place, but they're still adoptable."

CHAPTER
TWELVE

"We are free to choose our paths, but we can't choose
the consequences that come with them."
—Sean Covey, *Seven Habits of Highly Effective Teens*

THE MANAGEMENT OF La Maison allowed the residents to use the phone in the hallway for personal calls. Since all the other residents were at work, and my job started the next day, it was the perfect opportunity to phone Val.

I needed to hear her voice after my meeting with the case worker, Tammy Davis. "Hi, Val. I wanted to call you before I start working."

"Are you serious? You're working? Why?"

I started to answer but Val couldn't wait. "I don't understand. Where are you working?"

"At a restaurant."

"At a restaurant? What restaurant? I'm confused." She paused and I imagined her shaking her head with a million and one questions. "Start from the beginning. Don't leave anything out."

"Promise me you won't tell Mama I called you."

"Of course not. Now I'm more confused. What's going on? Did something happen?"

I spent the next half hour telling Val about the home, the job, and the reason why my mother sent me away from home to live in La Maison. Her voice grew taut. "Didn't Mama discuss any other options with you?"

"Other options? Like?"

"Like staying home and then placing the baby for adoption."

I laughed dryly. "Have you met our mother?"

"You've got a point there. But what about staying with me?"

"Are you kidding? Mama would never agree. In fact, she knew you would suggest that."

"Oh Nikki. I'm so sorry. I worry about you. You're so young. You're a child. Why couldn't she think about you for a change and at least consider an abortion?"

"That was a no-no from the start. Besides, I didn't think that's possible here."

"In Canada? Anything is possible if you can afford the cost. I've even heard that there are some dependable physicians who will perform an abortion for cash."

"That wouldn't make a difference to Mama."

"I'm so sorry, Nikki. It's going to be hard no matter what. Some people say that having an abortion is tough. Mentally. To tell the truth, I don't think you would survive one."

I made a noise with my throat, uncertain as to how to respond.

Val sighed deeply, her voice breaking as she continued. "But, Nikki, I have no idea what putting up a child for adoption will do to you. I'm concerned. I'm worried. Why did Mama have to send you so far away? You're all alone. No one to talk to, no one to help you. What was she thinking? I'm so mad at her."

Me too.

I heard Val take a few loud, calming breaths before changing the subject. "Are you going to be at the home for all those months?"

"I can choose to go home on weekends and holidays, but you live too far, so I'll just stay here. I'll phone you when I can. March isn't too far away, but I'll miss you." Silent tears ran unchecked down my face.

"I think that's a good decision. Mama would be preaching the evils of sin if you went home. I'm so sorry I can't visit you. The baby is due any day now." She continued after a brief pause. "You know, it had occurred to me that Eli could visit you, but on second thought, I don't think that's a good idea."

"He would lose it."

"Yeah. He's very protective of you and would tear the school apart look-ing for the guy who got you pregnant. Give me the address of La Maison. I'll send you a care package that will include some of my maternity clothes. But promise me one thing, Nikki."

"What?"

"That you'll call me every week just to check in. You know how much I worry about you. Promise?"

"Promise. I love you."

• • •

The restaurant was within a ten-minute walk from La Maison and occupied the end unit of a strip plaza with five commercial spaces. A convenience store was at the other end. Next to it was a hair salon, a pharmacy, and then a vacant space. I stood for a few minutes looking at the restaurant sign, "Good Eats," that promised to serve up hearty Canadian meals for a late breakfast and an early dinner from Mondays to Saturdays. Then, as instruct-ed, I turned and made my way to the side entrance, muttering along the way, "No rest for the wicked."

Working at the restaurant reminded me of grade 8. Everyone looked at me, grunted a greeting, then promptly forgot I existed. A tired-looking wom-an explained my chores and directed me to my station. "Don't be late and make sure you finish your work before you leave. There is no time for idle chatter." Her glance raked over me. "Hmm. Make sure you eat. I don't want you passing out. Anyway, just do your work and I'll be happy."

She didn't have to give me those instructions more than once. Washing dishes and cleaning the floors didn't require making conversation with the other workers. I only took short breaks to eat between washing the constant stream of dirty dishes and keeping the floor clean. I arrived at the restaurant at 10:00 a.m. and left at 6:00 p.m. except on Wednesdays, when I started at 1:00 pm. Whenever I worked at the restaurant, I kept my head down, did my work, and then returned to the home.

I went straight to bed when I returned to La Maison, too tired on some days to even watch television, falling asleep as soon as my head hit the pillow.

• • •

In early December, all the residents decided to remain at La Maison for Christmas. I received a care package from Val that included cash, personal items, lounge wear, and four of her maternity tops. My mother dropped off a bottle of sorrel drink and a small black cake with the supervisor. Although sharing them with the residents took away some of the sting of abandonment, my mother's action sent me into a deep depression.

The depression weighed me down for two days before I had a chance to meet with Tammy. I broke down as soon as I took a seat, crying uncontrollable for what seemed like hours while Tammy sat silently, handing me tissues. When my tears ran dry, I removed the pamphlet I had received from the doctor from my pocket and placed it in front of her.

Tammy took time to process the information, giving me the space to wipe away more tears. "Did something trigger a flashback?"

I shook my head. Tammy waited.

Taking a deep breath, I spoke in a quivering voice. "I'm finding it hard to deal with everything. It's just too much." I closed my eyes to keep from falling apart and wrapped my hands tightly around my body.

"That's a lot for anyone. Too much, I think, for you. Did you talk to someone after you experienced the sexual violence?"

"No. My mother and my doctor think I agreed. I have no one. My sister lives in Toronto."

Tammy touched my hand. "You don't have to go through this alone. I'm here for you."

I blew my nose and nodded.

"I'll gladly give you the time and the space you need while you're at La Maison. I'll help you with information, emotional support, and practical assistance. Are you open to counselling?"

I sighed. "Maybe later." I bit my lip, waiting for her to respond.

"I understand. In addition to working, you also have to deal with the pregnancy and placing your baby for adoption."

My heart thrummed insistently against my ribcage, underscoring the crowd of worries running helter-skelter through my mind. I slumped in the chair, my shoulders weighed down with heavy burdens.

"Nikki, you should know that you might experience emotional trauma after you leave here. I'll give you the information for a couple of rape crisis organizations and twenty-four-hour provincial crisis lines. They offer free and confidential support. But I strongly recommend counselling."

"Okay. Thank you." I couldn't think that far into the future. I found it exhausting.

CHAPTER
THIRTEEN

"You care so much you feel as though
you will bleed to death with the pain of it."
—J.K. Rowling, *Harry Potter and the Order of the Phoenix*

INITIALLY, I THOUGHT it best to be emotionally detached from my baby, since I'd be putting him or her up for adoption. But my heart softened after I heard the baby's heartbeat for the first time. I waited impatiently for Anna to get home that evening.

"How did it sound?"

"It was fast but quiet. It's a faint sound, like when you put a clock under your pillow. You can hardly hear it, but you know it's there."

"Really?"

"Yeah. The sound reached my heart. I felt the touch. That's when we bonded. Does that make sense?"

Anna smiled and nodded.

"My heart started beating faster just knowing that I was responsible for creating life, for bringing a human into the world. That's something no one can take from me. That scared me. But I also felt tenderness, love, and a sudden desire to protect the baby. That must be what they call motherly love. A love that will forever bind us." A solitary tear escaped. "What am I going to do? What will happen when that bond gets broken?"

"I don't have an answer for you simply because I haven't been in your situation. We both know that you have no choice but to place the baby for adoption. Hearing the heartbeat complicates everything for you. However, you'll need to be strong emotionally. It's going to be an uphill emotional battle. What matters now is how you deal with the situation."

"I don't know where to start. Will you help me?"

"Of course. Let's put our heads together and see what solutions we can think of."

I nodded, too choked to utter a word. We talked about different options to help me express what I was going through. When we exhausted all the options, Anna gently reminded me, "*He gives power to the faint, abundant strength to the weak*" (Isaiah 40:29).

Later that evening, I retired early to reflect on what had happened, and I used one of the options Anna and I spoke about to communicate with my baby.

> My Dearest Baby,
>
> This is the first time I'm expressing on paper what I feel and what I think. I'm a bit uncertain what to write or how to say what I feel, but I'm writing from my heart, so I'm sure you'll understand.
>
> I've never written a letter to anyone. All I know is that my friends back home always started a letter to their pen pal with "Dear So and So." But you are so much more than a pen pal. You're part of me. Me, little Nikki Robinson. I still can't take it all in. Anyway, what I mean to say is that you are my dearest.
>
> So, my dearest baby, first things first. I'm giving you a name. I can't keep calling you Baby. If you're male, I'll call you Joel. Joel was my grandfather's name. My father's father. I loved him. I'm not very tall, but Grandpa was over six feet, smart, and everyone in the village liked and respected him. He always patted my head and called me his beautiful princess. If you're female, I'll name you Brianna. Brianna was my best friend on the island.
>
> Yes. I was born on an island. I only came to this country, to Canada, a year ago, but I have no friends. The kids

at my new school are mean. One is especially horrible, but that's a story for another day. I made a mistake and I became pregnant. But do you know what? You're the best thing that happened to me. And now I can't even keep you.

You see, my dearest, I'm too young to keep you. I understand in my head, yet I have a tough time accepting it in my heart. I have no family at the place where I was sent to give birth. It's very lonely.

So why am I writing to you? My one friend, Anna, suggested that writing a letter to you might help me deal with the emotional upheaval in my life. I hope that writing to you is what some adults would say is a form of therapy. It's the only way I can think of that will help me deal with the pain of putting you up for adoption before I even know you. This is also the only way I know of expressing my love, even though I know you'll never get to read my letters. This might sound strange, but I love you without knowing you and even knowing that I'll never hold you.

The reality of this unplanned pregnancy means my entire future has changed.

How can I live after losing part of myself? I'm now faced with the reality that I must break this bond after you're born. Right now, I feel that doing so will slowly kill me.

Dearest child, I'm not strong enough; I'm not brave enough. I'll write when the loneliness, grief, pain, and despair become unbearable. I'll write everything I'm thinking and everything I'm feeling. I'll write to remember you through the years. I will write to survive, to live not knowing who you will become.

Always in my heart.

I did not sign the letter. It seemed too final.

• • •

I kept dreading the day when I would have to make the irrevocable decision. Tammy introduced the topic of adoption during every conversation, even talking more about the pros and cons of keeping the baby. Finally, she laid some papers on the table. "Nikki, it's time. As your legal guardian, your mother has already given her consent. It's time for you to sign."

Time had a way of running out on me, and I was grateful for Tammy's patience. She had generously given me the space to come to terms with what I had to do. I looked at the adoption papers and shivered, not from the cold December air seeping in through the window but from the cut I was about to inflict on my heart. I was only asked to sign my name. She didn't provide other information.

My eyes glazed over as I reached for the pen that turned into a knife in my hand. My entire body became numb. I disassociated myself, leaned forward, and signed my name.

Forgive me, my child.

My loss threatened to swallow my trust and remaining joy, and nothing felt steady. I became lost in my own sadness. I only found strength by mentally repeating, over and over, *Courage, courage, courage.*

Later that evening, Anna understood my pain and sat with me in silence. I needed her strength to make it up the stairs before crawling into bed.

CHAPTER
FOURTEEN

"No there's no way not to suffer. But you try all kinds of
ways to keep from drowning in it, to keep on top of it,
and to make it seem—well, like, you. Like you did something, all right, and now you're suffering for it."
—James Baldwin, *Sonny's Blues*

THAT EVENING, SLEEP eluded me, since I was unable to relate to the entire
process. My head and my heart were at war. Heaving a deep sigh, I sat up
and reached for a pen and paper before pulling the blanket off the bed and
going to sit in the chair by the window. I looked out and up to see stars twin-
kling in the night sky, secure in the knowledge that they kept me company. I
turned my thoughts to the baby.

My Dearest Brianna/Joel,

I signed the adoption paper today. Every stroke
became a dagger stabbing at my heart. Every stroke
slowly and painfully killing me. I hated my weakness. I
hated the fact that I was powerless. I had to do what my
mother wanted. I had to do what was expected of me. I'm
so sorry. I hope that someday you'll understand.

But I had no choice. I had to sign the papers, and
the only way I could do so was to detach myself from the
process. I remembered shutting my eyes tightly when I

wanted to avoid seeing something painful. This is what happened today. But it was a million times more painful. I had to shut down my entire body so I could place you for adoption.

You see, my dearest, I have no support from my mother. My pregnancy horrified her and brought her shame. She hid me away, so I know she would never help me raise you. The mere idea of her child having a child is unthinkable. It's just not something society would expect to happen in a good and decent home. I'm sure if she could, she would have sent me back to the island and disowned me. That's the reason why I must give you to a family who can raise you. Besides, I know what it's like to have a father growing up and then not having him around after a few years. I want you to grow up with a mother and father who'll love you. I want a better life for you. I love you and will always love you.

I'm just fourteen, and some people say I look twelve. I can't cook very well, and I couldn't even take care of a goldfish. My sister gave me one as a surprise gift and it died because I didn't do something right. Yes, I have a sister. Your aunt's name is Valerie, but we call her Val, and your uncle's name is Eli, which is short for Elijah. Therefore, if I can't take care of a goldfish, I certainly couldn't take care of you. I want you to live. I only want what's good for you. Please don't judge me harshly. I hope that you can forgive me when you're older.

Yes, I'll place you for adoption, but you're part of me. That I'll never forget. I'll never forget you. Never. I'll carry you forever in my heart. For as long as I live.

Everyone talks about going back to the life I had, but how can I? I'm not the same person. I can't just wipe the slate clean and start over.

My dearest, I can't protect you from the harsh realities of this world, but do you know what I'm going to do? At least, I hope I can find the strength to do it. I'm going to have a birthday party for you every year. It will just be me, but I'll have a cake with candles and a card. I know that's something you would like, because I love birthday parties. Anyway, I'll have to think about what to do about the gifts. Maybe we won't have gifts.

I hope you don't have to wait too long before you're adopted. I hope that you get to go to good people who will love you. I hope that you grow up strong, stay in school, and are good to your mother and father. I got pregnant with you when I was in grade 8, but it would be great if you can go to university. I have hope.

I'll pray for the blessing from Grandpa Joel on your birth and ask him to watch over you because I can't. Pregnancy changed my life, and hearing your heartbeat became an unbroken bond. You will always be with me.

One thing I learned was that a person will do crazy things to be seen and loved. I hope that you're never that lonely, never that desperate.

Always in my heart.

Tears fell on the paper, smudging some of the words.

CHAPTER
FIFTEEN

"Children and mothers never truly part, bound together
by the beating of one another's heart."
—Charlotte Gray

THE FOLLOWING JANUARY turned bitterly cold with freezing rain, making it challenging for me to walk to the restaurant. It became hard to breathe in the freezing air, and I was afraid of falling and hurting the baby. The ten-minute walk turned into a thirty-minute ordeal, and thankfully the restaurant manager decided that it was time for me to stop working at the restaurant. The La Maison house administrator agreed, and I started working in the kitchen at La Maison the next day.

In addition to peeling vegetables like carrots and potatoes, I grated what needed to be grated and washed whatever needed to be washed. Although this new arrangement offered relief from the elements, my back started hurting and I was constantly tired.

At the beginning of March, I began to stress about giving birth. Anna tried to distract me, but when she wasn't around, my mind went haywire. I created lots of scenarios around delivering the baby, about the pains I was sure to endure, and about how I would feel afterwards. As a result, I had trouble sleeping and the days and nights seemed endless.

I knew I wouldn't see Anna after I had the baby, but I had the opportunity to let her know how grateful I was for her love and support. She'd made my stay at the home bearable. Even though our paths would never cross again, she would always have a special place in my heart.

• • •

I didn't have to worry about knowing when I would go into labour. A few weeks later, around mid-March, I opened my eyes one morning and debated whether to sneak in another five minutes in bed. I closed my eyes from an achy feeling all over before feeling a strong cramping in my stomach all the way to my back.

Thinking the cramping was due to the restless night, I got out of bed, hoping the pain would subside after I walked around the room. But I paused every few moments to double over from the intensity of the pain.

Half an hour later, I stopped abruptly, my eyes opening wide, my voice shaky with awe and excitement at the revelation. "Oh, my goodness! Am I in labour?" My heart started beating faster. "I'm in labour. Time to have the baby." I placed my hand on my stomach. "I'm scared." I took a deep breath. "But you'll be okay. I promise."

However, motherhood had to wait. Not only was my labour hard, but loneliness also made an appearance amid all the pain. Loneliness and fear. The same fear I felt on my first day of high school. The walls crowded and pressed into me, competing with painful panic and loneliness. I had to steel myself enough to push through both. I had no one. Not on my first day of high school and not now. "Why, Brian? Why? Was it because I'm different? Was I an experiment? I only wanted a friend. I hate you! I hate this. This is too much pain." My mother had hidden me away and temporarily forgotten I existed. "Why, Mama? Why didn't you prepare me for this? Why did you leave me all alone? Why don't you like me?"

The pain became fierce. I could only get through it by giving myself a pep talk. "I can do this. I'll get through this. Lots of women don't have friends or family. But I'll never, never do this again."

I lost count of the time, of the number of hours before I was told the baby was in distress.

Another sharp pain. "Distress?" My heart hurt.

"You can't have a safe delivery on your own. We have to help you."

I groaned. "How?" I found it difficult to speak because it was hard to find my breath.

"We're going to do an emergency Caesarean." I only heard the word *emergency*. I didn't remember any previous mention of Caesarean. The tears escaped and ran down the side of my face. The nurse's words reassured me. "Don't worry. We'll put you to sleep."

Everything blurred together as the nurse moved me to a stretcher and along a passage. I kept my eyes closed from the confusion and the pain. Amidst all the activity, I blinked back a few threatening tears to notice several people in scrubs hustling about the cold, sterile room. The flurry of activity and the unfamiliar medical words temporarily distracted me from my fear and pain. Words didn't register.

Please do what you must do quickly. Please, please get my baby out safely.

I moaned, and in the height of the pain, I felt the needle. I was asleep within moments.

• • •

The nurse looked at me after the birth of my baby. "You have a healthy baby boy. Do you want to hold him."

I shook my head. "No. I can't."

She murmured. "I understand. He'll be in the newborn nursery. I'll take you back to your room." She gave me a compassionate look before wheeling me out of the recovery room.

No one told me what to expect after I gave birth to a child I couldn't keep. I stood in the darkness, with my baby ripped from me, with empty arms, unable to prevent the emptiness spreading into my soul. I had a child I could not hug, a baby with whom I could not bond. Would his body feel warm against mine? Would he feel soft and cuddly in my arms? The loss became unbearable. What's the purpose of my life? Here was irrefutable proof that I would never be a mother to my child. My heart shattered into a million pieces, causing me to lose my way and become numb with grief.

Tears flowed freely down my face while I screamed inside.

This hurts too much. I long to hold him. But how can I put him up for adoption if I hold him?

I turned and buried my face in the pillow. My body trembled from my loss, grief, and pain. The screams stuck in my throat and turned into a river of tears. I wept uncontrollably. I wept for all that I would miss, for all that I would never know. I cried a flood of tears. I cried until the tears ran dry, leaving me physically and mentally numb.

Hours later, I rolled over and stared up at the ceiling. I became spiritually frozen and could only whisper. "Lord, I heard how you helped people carry their burden. Lord, my burden is heavy. Too heavy. I've fallen. Hard. I need your strength. Strength to go on living. To carry this load. My faith is young. It's weak. The pain is unbearable. You know my heart. Can you help me? But you'll have to carry me—me and my burden—from now on."

The distant memory of the poem "Footprints in the Sand," which I enjoyed hearing Anna read to me, lingered in my subconscious.

Desire and motherly instinct pulled me toward my baby. I took the first step. Although moving around was hard, I clasped my hands together, took a few quieting breaths, and had a one-sided conversation. "I wonder who he looks like? I can't stop thinking about him. Is he scrawny? Is he crying a lot? He's so close. I must see him." I longed to see the face of my baby and to watch him breathe. However, as I drew closer and closer to the nursery, every muscle in my body tensed, every step laboured, matching the beating of my heart as the blood pounded in my head.

I stood observing the three babies in bassinets through the nursery window facing out to the hospital corridors. Later, I found out that the other newborn babies were with their mothers. From the first visit, I knew the only one with curly black hair and a light brown complexion belonged to me. "Oh! You're so beautiful! You're wrapped so snuggly! So cuddly! You look happy and healthy. I'm glad you're not crying. I wonder how much you weighed. My heart breaks. I'll never know how it feels to cradle you in my arms."

Somehow, I found the strength to visit my baby a couple of times. I whispered every time I saw him. "You're so perfect! How can I say goodbye?"

On my last visit, I placed a palm on the glass and said in a broken voice. "Joel, who will you become?" I looked at the other babies before returning my gaze to Joel. "I hope you don't have to wait too long before you're adopted."

I continued in a broken voice with tears streaming down my face. "So long, my sweet child. I'll see you every time I look at my face in the mirror. Every beat of my heart will be like the beating of your heart. I will love you with every breath I take."

I turned, wrapped the heavy shawl of grief around my shoulders, and walked away but didn't look back. The time had come to leave Joel, to leave the hospital, to begin my mourning.

CHAPTER

SIXTEEN

"Only time and tears take away grief; that is what they are for."
—Terry Pratchett, *I Shall Wear Midnight*

THE CONSTANT EMOTIONAL upheavals wore me down and sapped my energy. The day I returned home turned out to be another emotionally draining one in my life. Questions assailed me while I waited for my mother. How would she treat me? What was she going to do? How would she explain my return? I didn't have to wait long.

My mother surprised me by getting out of the car to hug me. Then she stepped back, casting a critical glance over me. "You're looking well." The unspoken word *considering* hung suspended in the air with the pause. "You've lost weight. We're going to have your favourite meal for dinner. Breadfruit and saltfish."

On the ride home I tuned out my mother, who continued to talk about this food and that food, about the people at church, and about Val's life. When Marian started to gush about her grandson, I didn't realize there were places in my heart that could still feel intense pain. "You should see your nephew. He's so adorable. Wait till I show you the pictures. God has indeed blessed me with a beautiful grandchild."

Sticking a knife in my heart would be less painful.

My mother glanced briefly at me when she ran out of words to describe her joy. Then she cleared her throat. "Ahh. Do you remember George?"

I nodded.

He hates me.

"Good. He's living at the townhouse now."

My wide eyes mirrored confusion when I turned my head to look at my mother.

She shrugged. "Don't look at me like that. The house felt empty after your brother moved out." She spoke a bit faster. "The house is too big anyway. I'm planning on marrying George, and we'll move to a smaller place as soon as you're settled."

I turned my head to stare out the window. A shiver ran down my spine despite the heat in the car. Tears hovered on my eyelids. I tried not to blink, but they spilled over anyway.

• • •

I phoned my sister the next day. My knuckles turned white as I gripped the phone. My voice came out breathless. "Sorry, I couldn't talk a lot when I was away, but I'm home now."

Val's voice sounded like music to my ear. "Nikki! You're home! So good to have you back." I heard the joy in her voice. "Hope the drive home wasn't too bad."

"Bearable. Mama kept gushing about her role as a grandmother." A pain squeezed my chest, forcing me to lean against the closest wall. "How's everyone?"

"Your nephew, Greg, is doing great. Growing fast. Can't wait for you to meet him."

I choked.

Please, not now.

I took a deep breath. "Neither can I." The tears silently rolled down my face.

"Come by in the summer. Okay?"

"Okay."

• • •

I cried myself to sleep every night, sniffled all day, and occasionally burst into tears until my mother had enough. "Nikki, you must stop this. You're upsetting George, and I can't take it anymore." Her lips tightened as she adjusted the front of her new floral silk kimono robe, smoothing her hair neatly arrayed in a bun.

I swiped my hand across my wet cheeks and blew my nose. With eyes still puffy from crying, I looked at my mother, then down at my hands. "Sorry." Raising my head halfway, I cleared my throat. "Did you tell him?"

"Of course I told him." My mother gave me a side glance before sucking her teeth.

"Oh." My heart sank.

She shrugged her shoulders. "He said he understood."

I mumbled under my breath, "Then why is he avoiding me like the plague? Who am I? Jezebel?" I recalled the older church ladies on the island standing with folded arms as they frowned on any young woman who dared to show too much skin or walk in a provocative manner, labelling them as Jezebels. But I consoled myself with a delicious thought that maybe George might have gotten someone pregnant and ran away to Canada to avoid taking any responsibility. The thought caused me to hiccup loudly.

"What did you say?"

"Nothing."

My mother shook her head. "Child, you're driving me crazy with all this crying. You just can't sit around all day feeling sorry for yourself. You need to find something to do. Work will take your mind off what happened."

"Yes, ma'am."

She folded her arms. "Another thing. You have terrible acne. Call the doctor to get some medication for it and for your dry, scaly skin. Nobody will hire you if you're constantly scratching." She was referring to the dermatological conditions I developed after giving birth.

Adjusting the front of her robe again, she continued. "Now that you're back, you must think about continuing your education."

My head nodded automatically.

Can't it wait?

She continued, "Since you can't go back to your old school, I'll write a letter to your school board to apply for you to return to another school."

"Yes, ma'am."

My mother's voice became lighter. "But I'll leave the rest up to you after I've heard from them. Based on their response, you'll have to meet with the principal and register for the new school year."

She didn't expect an answer. Every corner of my brain seemed to be full of worry, full of questions, full of uncertainty. The bombardment wore me down, and I couldn't summon the energy to respond. It became easier to become a programmed robot following all her directions.

● ● ●

Two weeks later, my mother found a job for me. "I asked around at church to see if anyone knew of job openings, and of course Mrs. Carmen said you could work for her at the restaurant."

"What do I have to do?"

My mother waved a hand in the air. "She mentioned cleaning. I swear the woman would create a job just for you."

I nodded.

Later in the evening, I called Val in a panic after finding hair in the sink. "Val, my hair! My hair! What do I do?"

"Slow down, Nikki. What about your hair?"

"I'm losing it. In clumps. I have patches. On my scalp. What's happening?"

Val consoled me. "I'm so sorry, Nikki. There's no need to panic. You've been through a lot. I'm sure it's from all the stress."

"Oh. That's a relief. But Val, I just got a job. How can I work like that?"

"Did you mention your hair problem to Mama?"

"Are you kidding? No."

"Okay. Don't worry. A hairdresser can help."

"Is there one here I can go to?"

"Sure. I did hear of a new Black hairdresser on King Street. Let me find out the address and make an appointment for you. I'll explain everything to her, but still talk to her. She'll take care of you." She paused. "How are you doing otherwise?"

My voice broke. "They lied."

"Who lied?"

"They all said it would be easy."

"Oh Nikki!"

CHAPTER
SEVENTEEN

"It's like I have this large black hole in my brain and it's
sucking the life out of me. The answers are in there so I
sit for hours and stare. No matter how hard
and long I look, I only see darkness."
—Kate McGarry, *Pushing the Limits*

AFTER MY HAIR appointment, I stared at my reflection in the mirror. I recalled
cringing when the hairdresser cut my hair. In my subconscious, it was as if
someone took a pair of scissors to methodically cut away the last remnants
of my old life to make way for the start of a different future. What sort of
future awaited me? The new haircut exposed me to the world, making me
appear vulnerable and fragile. So many cracks! I had to get used to the new
me, to the girl with a short afro, sad eyes, and a serious face. Time to step
into my new reality.

Mrs. Carmen's joy at seeing me included wrapping me in a tight hug.
"Nikki! Child, I'm so happy to see you." She held me at arm's length to
examine me and then pulled me back into her embrace.

I wanted to cry. I wanted to remain in the comfort of Mrs. Carmen's
embrace but couldn't. I nodded wordlessly, certain that my eyes shone with
unshed tears.

Mrs. Carmen continued. "So sorry about what happened with your
mother. We missed you. We were all praying for you. Now, I'm delighted
you'll be helping us in the restaurant." She raked a glance over me. "Your
eyes are full of pain. Too much I would think for someone so young. The
stress of whatever happened last year changed you. You're different. Your

new hairstyle makes you look younger and more vulnerable. But it suits you." She shook her head. "No matter. You're back now." She smiled. "We need to fatten you up. The wind can blow you away. I hope you'll have your meals at the restaurant."

I gave her a ghost of a smile for her enthusiasm. "Thanks, Mrs. Carmen. Thanks for the job. For everything. It's good to be back. It's good to see you too." I loved this woman. She looked out for me. My guardian angel.

Her laugh twinkled. "Mrs. Carmen is such a mouthful. You can call me Aunty if it's easier for you or if it's something you'd like."

I grinned. "Thank you, Aunty."

However, I continued to keep my distance from everyone else. I didn't speak unless someone spoke to me. I grew extremely sad and very lonely because I only shared my feelings with my sister, who lived miles away in the city.

● ● ●

My mother didn't nag me about registering for school, but her eyes followed my every move and they spoke volumes. Therefore, a week after starting to work at the Bistro, I registered for the new school year at a different school. However, the principal stuck to the decision made by the school board. "We didn't think you needed to meet with other staff members. But I want to stress that we're taking you back because of your age."

I nodded.

"One of the conditions is that you attend different classes."

"Different classes?"

"Yes. It's the same grade, but you'll be in a non-academic group."

"I see."

"You missed an entire academic year, and we believe this is better for you. You can't seem to focus, leading us to believe that you have little or no interest in higher education. But we're here to ensure that you obtain your high school diploma. You'll be given the tools to help you find a job that will give you the means to support yourself after you graduate. Any questions?"

I asked timidly, "Can I apply for college?"

The principal barked out an incredulous laugh. "I don't see that happening." She shrugged. "But you can always see Mr. Monroe, the guidance counsellor."

CHAPTER
EIGHTEEN

"The dreams we are chasing and the reality that is chasing us are always parallel; they never meet."
— Ai Yazawa

I ALWAYS THOUGHT the principal would be the one to steer me along the
right educational path. Would Mr. Monroe tell me something different? I
knew in my heart that it was a useless exercise to see him, but I needed
someone to explain what moving to a non-academic group entailed.

Mr. Monroe cleared his throat. "So you're streamed to the non-academic group."

"What does streaming mean?"

"Academic streaming. It's a process whereby the school system divides
students into separate groups based on their perceived ability and/or prior
achievements."

"Who gets streamed in the academic group?"

"Well, in the academic groups, the lessons and resources are focused
on skill development with an emphasis on autonomy and critical thinking.
It's a fast-paced learning environment for students who want to attend university."

"But I wanted to attend university."

"Let me check your record." He accessed my file on his computer.
"It says here that the principal suspended you during your first year at
your former school and expelled you at the start of the second year." He

sighed. "This isn't looking good for you. I'm sorry, but that's the school's plan for you."

"I see. What type of work will I be suited for after I graduate?"

"Well, there are four areas—construction, industrial, transportation, and service." Mr. Monroe leaned back in his chair, using his fingers as he checked them off.

"Oh. Does that mean I can only go into the service sector?"

"Well, that would be my guess. You would be hard pressed to meet the requirements of the other sectors."

"Can you give me an idea of the career opportunities in the service industry?"

"Well, let's see." He paused, tilting his head to the right as if to pull his thoughts from the air. "There are a few. Off the top of my head, I would include cleaning services, cook, dishwasher, cashier, restaurant or super-market worker, warehouse worker, home support, or customer service."

I said in a weary voice. "Oh. Okay. Thanks." My heart sank at the options.

My past was ever before me. It was as though I walked one step behind it as it touched and painted my life a distinct colour. A grey colour. I had no choice but to follow and adjust to the drab new world. In this new world, the colour only covered a limited area, but I only had to lift my head to see the rest of the world awash with vibrant colours like green, red, yellow, and lavender.

My heart longed for the life I'd had before. My shoulders drooped. First, I needed to graduate. I dragged my feet as I left the office, still confused by the academic streaming process.

● ● ●

Two days later, I phoned Val. "Can you tell me why the school system has two types of educational groups?"

"Oh no! I hoped they didn't stream you into a non-academic group."

"Yes, they did."

"Was the guidance counsellor of any help?"

"Some. What do you know?"

"Not much. And the little I know is not encouraging."

"It's okay. I need to know."

CHAPTER EIGHTEEN

"Okay. I know it's not the place you want to be if you want to learn or if you have plans to go to college or university. I know that other students and teachers look down on those who are streamed. One of my friends got streamed because they thought he was 'slow.' He hated the atmosphere in the classes. He found it negative. It made him feel as though he'd done something wrong. He also said the schoolwork was boring and repetitious."

"What happened to your friend?"

"Although he was smart, the streaming was a blow to his self-esteem. He couldn't make the adjustment. He dropped out."

"Oh, sorry to hear that. Did he tell you anything else?"

"Yes. He mentioned that there's also a stigma associated with streamed students. It's that stigma that makes it harder to find work after graduation. He claimed that streamed students are disadvantaged."

"Do you mean labelled?"

"Yeah. And worse. I've even heard it referred to as the dummy classes."

"Was I streamed because I got pregnant?"

"That's why you got expelled. It's hard for me to say, but the system saw you as irresponsible and decided that streamed classes were best for you. From what my friend told me, the system would have low expectations of you. But I hope you prove them wrong. I'll be your biggest cheerleader as you fight to stay in school, as you struggle to graduate. You can do it, Nikki. Remember, you are not irresponsible. You're a fighter."

"I'll try to remember that." I asked after a pause, "Any idea of the other types of students who are streamed?"

"Sorry, Nikki, I don't know."

"Okay. Do you know if I can move back to the academic group?"

"I heard that's rare. My friend tried. He said even accessing post-secondary education and training is an uphill battle."

"Then how can the system expect us to stay motivated knowing the future that awaits us?"

"It's going to be tough, but you're strong and I know you'll graduate. I'm here for you." She paused. "Did you tell Mama?"

"Yes. Yesterday."

"And?"

"Her exact words were 'What did you expect? Academic streaming is your punishment for committing such a sin. I wanted you to attend university or college. I wanted a better life for you. But how did you repay me? By throwing everything away. Child, you're lucky the school system even took you back.' Then she turned her back on me." My voice cracked. I couldn't hold back the tears.

"Sometimes Mama can be so thoughtless and her words hurtful. She could have advocated for you to stay in the academic stream. Sorry, Nikki."

I asked, "Why doesn't she like me?" Because I knew she couldn't answer my burning question—did she want me?

"I really can't be certain. But I think it's because Daddy adored you the most. You're the youngest and that's expected, but Eli and I think she's tougher on you because of that special bond."

My heart sank. I closed my eyes, becoming stuck in the darkness of my mind, unable to move for a long time.

CHAPTER
NINETEEN

"Every day the clock resets. Your wins don't matter.
Your failures don't matter. Don't stress on what was,
fight for what could be."
—Sean Higgins

TWO MONTHS AFTER I started working at the Bistro, I overheard some of the workers talking about the room above the restaurant. Wanting more information, I approached Mrs. Carmen. "Aunty, I heard that the room upstairs is available for rent."

"Yes, it is. Do you know someone who needs a place to stay?"

"Yes, Aunty. Me."

Mrs. Carmen's glance sharpened. "Oh! I thought you lived at home."

"Yes, but I'm looking for a place."

Mrs. Carmen nodded. "I understand. So it's still not working out with you and your mom?"

I skirted answering the question. "Mama and George are planning to get married. I don't want to be in their way." I looked at Mrs. Carmen with earnest eyes. "So will you rent it to me?" Not waiting for a response, I pressed forward my case. "I'll continue to work here when school starts in September. You can take the rent money from my pay."

Mrs. Carmen sighed. "It's okay, child. I understand. Come. I'll show you the room."

I stood inside the doorway and let my gaze wander around the room. Light streamed in from the window to illuminate the head of a twin bed resting against the wall on my right. I caught a glimpse of the bathroom through the open door at the far end of the wall. Across from the door, I observed a writing desk and chair and a unit with a small fridge and a microwave. To my left, a couch was on one side of the window, and an armchair on the other side closer to the door.

My eyes lit up as I turned toward Mrs. Carmen. "It's perfect. I like it."

Mrs. Carmen slowly let her gaze travel from the room to me. "It suits you. I have an old television you can use if you don't have one."

I only nodded. My emotions were too close to the surface.

Mrs. Carmen gently touched my arm. "You can have the room for as long as you like." She smiled. "You can move in on the first of September."

I slumped with relief.

● ● ●

Arriving home an hour later, I opened the door with a flourish, a river of happiness rushing through my veins and displayed on my face for all to see. The food smell drifted toward me, letting me know where to find my mother. In my enthusiasm, the words flew out from my lips when I burst into the kitchen. "I'm moving out on September first."

My mother's head snapped up displaying pursed lips and blazing eyes. She said in a shrilled voice. "You're what? Why you little ungrateful child. Where are your manners? No 'Good evening.' Nothing. Just the news that you're moving out. How am I supposed to take that?" Anger distorted her features.

The happy bubble popped so loudly that I automatically recoiled as if she had slapped me. My heart thumped painfully against the wall of my chest. I gulped. "Sorry. Good evening, Mama."

"I've done so much for you. George even said I did too much. He's right. You're just like your father. And now you're loudly proclaiming your intention."

"Did George say that?" I breathed deeply, wrapping my arms around my body.

CHAPTER NINETEEN

"Never mind what he said. The fact is you're moving out." She shook her head. "What will people say? I'll tell you what they'll whisper behind my back. They'll say I'm not happy you're back. They'll say my young daughter can't live in the same house with me. George will be annoyed at you."

I lowered my gaze to the floor.

Marian's nostrils flared and her jaws and lips got tense when I remained silent. Her voice grew louder. "So now you think you're a woman. Let me tell you, missy, having a child doesn't make you a woman." Did she think I was a mistake? A mistake she couldn't have undone.

I clenched my fists to help still my trembling hands.

She hates me.

My mother dismissed my attempt at happiness without a second thought. Her words stabbed at my heart.

She didn't even ask about the apartment.

• • •

I called Val later that evening. "I wanted to let you know I'll be living somewhere else in September."

"Really? Why? Did Mama ask you to leave?"

"It's a bit cramped at home. It's better for everybody."

"I understand. Where are you going?"

"Mrs. Carmen has an apartment above her restaurant."

"That's good. She'll look out for you as if you're her own. But I still worry about you. Ahh, I hate to ask, but was it bad when you told her you're moving out?"

My voice broke. "She turned on me." I tried hard to keep the tears from falling.

"Oh no! I'm so sorry."

"I can't breathe in this place. I can't continue living under the same roof as Mama and George. I just hope I can survive until the end of August."

CHAPTER
TWENTY

"Grief is like the ocean; it comes on waves ebbing and
flowing. Sometimes the water is calm, and sometimes it
is overwhelming. All we can do is learn to swim."
—Vicki Harrison

MY JAW DROPPED when I entered the kitchen the morning after I made a mess declaring my intent to move. My mother and George sat stone-faced, with their cups of coffee on the kitchen table. Their presence was both unexpected and unnerving. I took a few calming breaths before I had the presence of mind to mutter, "Good morning."

My mother grunted but George stared at me without answering. I turned to look at them after pouring dry cereal in a bowl. Their narrowed eyes, flared nostrils, and tense postures made my hands shake, causing the contents of the bowl to spill onto the floor. "Sorry." My heart pounded as I bent to pick up the cereal.

My mother said, "That cereal cost money. You shouldn't waste it." George whispered something in a muffled voice and they both laughed.

George is a bad influence!

I lost my appetite and fled without looking at them. After that incident, I met with stony stares and hard eyes every time I saw them. Two days later, I found my items from the bathroom lined up outside my bedroom door. The message was louder than if it was shouted from the rooftops.

Because of the tense atmosphere at home, I spent most of my work-day pouring all my energy into making every spot shine at the Bistro. It was so clean that a person could eat off the floor. On the days when the Bistro opened for business, I got home late and went directly to my room. Sundays and Mondays found me either at the mall or hiding in my room.

The emotional upheaval and trauma I experienced throughout the past year came together to create the perfect storm in August. Would my mother acknowledge my birthday? Would she be civil toward me? She hadn't given me a card or a gift on my last birthday but had contributed to my lunch. This year I hoped for something. Anything.

When I returned in the evening, I looked for a card, for a token to cele-brate my special day, outside my bedroom door. Nothing. It was like a slap in the face.

Does she not want me?

The weight of grief grew too heavy for my shoulders. I stumbled. Reach-ing for support, I managed to crawl, dry-eyed, into bed. My mother's rejec-tion intensified my emotional pain. Tammy was right. Depression made an appearance. But this time loneliness, rejection, and isolation joined the existing pain from the shame of the sexual violence, from my pregnancy, and from the grief of putting my baby up for adoption.

I was weighed down and numb. I was weary. Lonely and living with a secret. I was fifteen years old. I wanted to die.

Every day I woke up and continued my life without my son. How was I supposed to live as though he was a mistake that could easily be forgotten? My mother believed he was an error in judgement I could wipe away like the writing on a chalkboard. Gone and forgotten. That could only happen in theory. It was easier said than done.

At nights, I stared up at the ceiling, trying to understand the complexi-ties of my life. Looking for answers in the silence, in the darkness. I had giv-en birth to a son but couldn't be a mother to him, while my mother pushed me away from her. I fumbled in the dark. I kept searching for a glimmer of light. I found hope. Hope was all I could cling to as I fought to keep my san-ity, counting the days, the hours, and the minutes until the end of August.

• • •

Thursday, September 1, 1983—an unforgettable date.

I woke up to a glorious day. Sitting up with a huge grin on my face, I looked at my belongings in bags and boxes and felt the weight of my grief lighten. Scrambling out of bed, I chose to surround myself with light as I got ready and waited for Eli.

Eli made two trips to the car before asking, "Is this it?"

"Yes."

He shook his head. "I thought women had lots of stuff. I had twice that amount when I moved out."

I shrugged my shoulders.

"Aren't you taking the things you used? Items like your bed linens and towels?"

I looked at him blankly, not knowing how to answer.

He went to the top of the stairs and called. "Mama, Nikki is taking her linens, towels, and whatever she used."

I heard loud grumbling before she responded. "Whatever. But only what she used."

I grinned from ear to ear packing those items.

• • •

I sang all the way to the apartment. But finding a television set, a microwave, pillows, and blankets made me dance and twirl around in my new space.

Eli laughed out loud. "Let me know what else you need. I'll take you shopping."

"You will? Thanks, Eli," I said, giving him a tight hug.

"You have the day off, so we'll have dinner at the Bistro later."

• • •

September was the month of change. I had shaken off the mental shackles imposed by my mother and George, but it was time to return to school, to face the restrictions on my education. The patches in my hair forced me to don a wig on my return. Getting to school and concentrating during class-es became an act of willpower. Val was right. Those of us in the non-ac-ademic stream were at a disadvantage. We were like sheep herded into a room and forgotten. We certainly didn't learn much. We did the minimum work. Our choice was simple—drop out of school or put in the time to graduate.

The first day was an eye-opener. Different classroom. Different teachers. The teacher, Mr. Lamb, looked bored, making no attempt at pretence. "Any questions?"

A timid voice asked, "Do we have the same curriculum as the others?"

Mr. Lamb looked at the nonexistent notes on his desk before replying. "This class is different. This is a basic level. We cover the same material—you'll get the same type of math, science, and English courses, just easier, less demanding. Everything is simple because we want you to graduate."

However, Mr. Lamb forgot to mention that the classes were less motivating. I looked around the classroom after the teacher assigned us to work on our own at the end of the first week. A few students with obvious education needs looked around helplessly with glazed, unfocused eyes. The rest of the students, including visible minorities and those speaking different languages, appeared in various stages of boredom. I tugged my grief around my shoulders and rested my head on the desk. The principal was right. Although I wanted to learn, I couldn't focus.

Am I a failure?

I groaned under my breath, "I hope I can make it to graduation."

All the students were in the same boat. We kept to ourselves. A month later, a new student, Mark Haynes, occupied the desk next to mine. During our lunch break, his look was non-judgemental when he said. *"Wah Gwaan?"*

My eyes popped wide open. "What?"

"Sorry. You're not Jamaican." He gave me a sheepish grin. "I asked 'What's up?' What brought you here?"

"Oh. Right." I laughed. "This is my rehabilitation plan after expulsion."

"Bummer."

"What about you?"

"Man, I just got to this place a few months ago. The teachers tell me they can't understand me. I tend to speak Patois when I'm stressed. But everyone talks so fast, it's confusing, and I found it hard to understand them. I couldn't keep up. Next thing I know, the principal sends me here because she claimed I'm too slow for the regular classes. That I'm not working hard enough. Man, I spoke with my cousins, and they tell me that after this, I'm only suited for manual work. *Raasclaat!*" He later explained that the Jamaican slang was an expression of anger and frustration.

"I know." We continued eating in silence.

After a moment, Mark said, "You know what I think?"

"What?"

"This streaming discriminates against us. It re-creates social inequality. I'll call it what it is—racism."

"Right!"

"And you know what else?"

"What?"

"I man from Jamaica. I'm a somebody. I have big plans. So after I graduate, I'll shake the dust from my feet, go to night school, and somehow I'll get to college if it's the last thing I do."

I believed him.

CHAPTER
TWENTY-ONE

"The human capacity for burden is like bamboo – far
more flexible than you'd ever believe at first glance."
—Jodi Picoult, *My Sister's Keeper*

I HAD TO develop mental toughness and resilience, but I couldn't bounce back from everything life had thrown my way. My days consisted of school during the days and working at the Bistro afterwards. But most nights, depression overwhelmed me as soon as I entered my apartment.

Sometimes I slumped on the floor and hugged a pillow—unable to cry, unable to think. Other times, the tears would flow as soon as I closed my door. Words mixed with tears. "Oh Lord … everything hurts … my head … my heart … my entire body. I need help. … I should get help. … It's too much … the pain. Please take it away … please … make it stop." Then I'd wrap the blanket around me and lay crumpled on the floor, waiting for sleep.

A month later, Val phoned to invite me to Thanksgiving dinner. I didn't have the energy to face my family. "This is a busy time at the Bistro," I said. But I promised to help out.

Val was sympathetic. "So sorry, Nikki. We'll miss you, but we'll see you for Christmas."

• • •

I started to panic soon after talking with Val. Christmas—it's supposed to be the most wonderful time of the year, a time to be jolly and happy. That was what everyone expected. I wasn't ready. My pain was still unbearable. How could I face my family? The next day, when my acne and eczema returned with full force, I called to renew my prescription.

The medication helped improve the way I looked. Luckily, I didn't have to be mentally alert at school and I could clean the Bistro with my eyes closed. Every day I walked past stores, unable to enter, unable to start my Christmas shopping. Donna's phone call toward the end of November brought me a bit of light and helped lessen my stress. "Hey, Nikki," she said, "I was at a Christmas bazaar and picked up an extra gift for Greg. I thought you could give it to him."

My legs buckled and I choked on my words. "Thanks, Donna. Thank you." The tears ran freely down my face.

• • •

In mid-December, I brought up the subject of Christmas with Val. "Are you having everyone over for Christmas?"

"Everyone?" she said. "Do you mean everyone in the family?"

"Yes. Like Mama and George."

"Oh! Right! Sorry, Nikki. I forgot to phone you. You won't believe it. Remember the ice storm we had last week?"

"Yes."

"Girl, George slipped on the ice. So he won't be here. Just us."

The day suddenly seemed brighter. "How is Mama getting to your place?"

"She said she would ask Eli."

There goes my ride.

"I see," I said. "I'll take the bus and return on Boxing Day."

"Wonderful. I'll have you for two days."

I mapped out a strategy to avoid my mother on Christmas Day. Luckily, she ignored me when she arrived. The muscles in my shoulders relaxed and I slumped against the closest wall, slowly letting out a breath.

So far, so good.

I took my cues from her action. Whenever she entered one room, I went to another, or I took the seat furthest away from her.

Somehow I survived Christmas.

• • •

My shawl of grief grew heavier at Christmas and turned into a cozy blanket on my son's first birthday in March. I stayed in bed that morning, enveloped in a cloud of pain and darkness. Was it March break? Was I supposed to be in school? Nothing mattered. I summoned enough energy to work one hour at the Bistro. Then, claiming to be unwell, I drank a cup of tea and returned to my apartment. I celebrated my son's first birthday by placing one candle on the slice of cake from the restaurant but couldn't eat it. I had no appetite. Grief and regret overwhelmed me, leaving me sad and withdrawn as I wondered what kind of couple, assuming it was a couple, had adopted Joel. What had become of him?

The ache grew in my chest.

> My Dearest Joel,
> You're one today. Happy birthday!
> I hope the couple who adopted you are good and caring people. People who will love you and take care of you. I only want you to be happy and healthy.
> I'm so sorry I missed, and will miss, some of the "firsts" in your life—crawling, first steps, first words, and so much more.
> Always in my heart.

• • •

The pain overrode my desire to write a lengthy letter. Choking on my tears, I sobbed for more than missed birthdays and celebrations. How could I explain the deep disappointment at missing his first birthday, his first words, smiles, and steps?

My face became puffy and swollen with grief. Hours passed before I fell asleep clutching the card to my heart.

• • •

My grief cloaked me. Although a smile covered a multitude of hurts, the turmoil within me forced me to improvise, to continually find ways to keep the grief from becoming visible. It was like fighting to keep water from seeping out through a container stretched to its limit. I kept my eyes shut every time I went to the hairdresser, but I lifted my head and tried to walk like a model every time I left my apartment. Every time I used a wig, people's admiring glances and smiles helped to keep the pain hidden.

But I also had to keep from falling apart. I remembered how my heart had raced at the thought of a new life growing within me. I remembered feeling overwhelmed with joy and happiness at my son's birth. Those memories now brought a sad smile to my face, but they weren't sufficient to keep the grief from seeping out, to keep me from falling apart. It wasn't enough to keep me from crying every night. It wasn't enough to keep sadness from drenching me to my core.

I received a temporary solution from one of my classmates in the streamed classes to keep the grief from spilling over. Mark Haynes turned to me during lunch. "Are you okay?"

"Yes. Why do you ask?"

"You're so quiet. You're here, but sometimes it seems like you're somewhere else. You look so sad, and you don't say much."

"Oh," I replied in dismay.

It shows! Does everyone know?

"It's okay. No need to panic. I don't think anyone else noticed. Anything I can do?"

Make the pain go away.

"Thanks. But I don't think so. Just personal stuff."

"Don't worry." His smile brightened my day. "I'll look out for you at school. I'll make it my personal mission to keep the sad look off your face when you're here."

My hand held my heart in place. "Oh Mark! That's so sweet. Thank you." Tears pooled but didn't fall.

"Hey! I want my buddy around. Yeah, I want you next to me when we graduate."

I gently touched his arm, giving him a brilliant smile. His ray of light brought me hope. It lightened my grief.

"We'll get through this together. Together we'll graduate."

● ● ●

The sun hid behind the clouds on graduation day. I sat next to Mark for the last time. Nudging him with a shoulder, I said, "I'll miss you."

"Me too."

"Thank you, Mark. I'm here today because of you."

He shook his head. "We made it. Together."

I nodded, and then we shared a few minutes of comfortable silence.

Mark spoke quietly. "Nikki, we needed each other to get through the tough times. We both had dark days. Everyone has dark days. Remember my mission?" He smiled at me. "You're my friend. I didn't want to get to the finishing line alone. I may not see you again, but I'll always remember your capacity to bounce back. Little sis, you're like elastic. You're stronger than you think. It will be a rough road ahead, but I believe in you. You'll get where you need to be. Eventually."

"Eventually! Thank you, Mark. For everything." Tears of gratitude escaped through the corners of my eyes.

Looking at my high school diploma later that evening, I asked it the many questions lurking in my mind. "How far will you get me? Where will you take me? What kind of future will I have? How will I survive? Who will help make the sadness invisible?"

Putting aside the diploma, with tears streaming down my face, I whispered, "Eventually is so far away." I wrapped my grief around me. "I don't want to die of a broken heart."

CHAPTER
TWENTY-TWO

"These days grief seems like walking on a frozen river;
most of the time he feels safe enough, but there is
always that danger he will plunge through."
—David Nicholls, *One Day*

AFTER GRADUATION, I continued working part-time in the restaurant while trying to find a full-time job. I applied for a job at retail stores, restaurants, fast food outlets, grocery stores, and convenience stores, but received rejection after rejection.

"Sorry, you don't have the experience we're looking for."

"Sorry, we have nothing available."

"Sorry, we're looking for someone with at least grade 11 math."

"Sorry, we need someone with more education."

Sometimes they told me the job was no longer available as soon as I walked through the door.

Months later, I applied for and accepted a job with a company contracted to clean residential and commercial properties. Although I worked independently, I was part of a team assigned to provide total building maintenance. That included providing janitorial services for a few medical facilities, cleaning services for assigned commercial properties, and interim cleaning for a handful of residential properties. Most calls for residential properties came from agents who wanted the properties cleaned before they listed the house for sale.

CHAPTER TWENTY-TWO

Since I didn't drive, I used public transportation to either meet a team member who drove to the location or to meet the team outside the building by an assigned time.

• • •

I always stopped at the restaurant after working for the cleaning company. Although Mrs. Carmen indicated that she wanted me to work only two evenings a week, I pushed for three but spent every evening at the restaurant. I had nowhere else to go. I had no one. I helped the other workers when it wasn't my time to work. I cleaned the floors. I washed dishes; I cleared tables. Anything to keep me from thinking, from remembering.

One evening Mrs. Carmen pulled me aside. "Nikki, dear, it breaks my heart that you're here night after night. Why don't we try something else to keep you occupied? Can you cook?"

"Some. I can make breakfast."

She laughed. "Would you like to learn how to make some of the dishes we serve here?"

"Yes, Aunty."

"Good. I'll talk with the cook, and he'll teach you."

"Thanks, Aunty," I said, a smile lighting up my face.

I eagerly anticipated my evenings at the Bistro. Everyone loved the cook, Mr. Benjamin, whom we called Mr. Benji. He started me off with learning to make appetizers, like soups and crab cakes, progressing to simple dishes, like ackee and saltfish, and eventually, he taught me how to make entrées, like jerk chicken, oxtail stew, and seafood-based meals.

However, Mrs. Carmen still wanted me to maintain a life outside of the restaurant. "Child, you're young. Go out. Enjoy yourself."

I only smiled, but the smile didn't reach my eyes. "Yes, Aunty."

Mrs. Carmen shook her head. "I worry about you. I hope and pray that you can escape those demons that plague you. I hope Isaiah 43:2 will remind you that God will carry you through the storm. I know He has a purpose for your pain and a reason for your struggle. Please don't give up. Trust Him."

• • •

I remained spiritually frozen for a long time because my primary request to God, to know the whereabouts and welfare of my son, had never been answered. But Mrs. Carmen's generosity and kindness nudged the door of my heart ajar, wide enough to let in a ray of God's merciful grace, with the hope that He would do the rest—removing the sting of past regret and my worry about the future.

Furthermore, I wanted to please Mrs. Carmen. She treated me like a daughter, and I didn't want to let her down. I attended service on Sundays but sat at the back of the church. I couldn't pray but found temporary comfort and peace in the Lord's presence. After the service, I greeted a few of the congregation and disappeared at the earliest opportunity, and before my mother and George made an appearance, to spend the rest of the day in my room.

However, there was no escaping my family. My mother married George Plummer in a small, quiet ceremony at the church. She wore an off-white skirt suit with embroidery embellishment and a rhinestone brooch, which she told us was a gift from George. A simple matching hat completed her look. The three of us and a few friends met at the restaurant for the reception. I treated George the same way he treated me and simply wished my mother well. She was in her element. Thankfully, she only had eyes for George, making it easier for me to keep out of her way.

Once a month Eli took me shopping and we had dinner at the restaurant. I spoke with Val every week and spent Christmas Day with her in Toronto. I loved my sister dearly but had to steel myself to be around my nephew, Greg. Every visit, every birthday and Christmas with Val became a daggered reminder that I lived with my child's absence. Every child's gift I bought and every hug I gave Greg proved bittersweet, impeding my healing progress.

CHAPTER
TWENTY-THREE

"Life doesn't get easier or more forgiving, we get stronger and more resilient."
—Steve Maraboli, *Life, the Truth, and Being Free*

I RECEIVED AN interesting phone call from Val just after I turned nineteen. "Daddy has been calling me." She paused, but I was too shocked to say anything. "The thing is, he wants to see you."

I said the first thing that popped into my head. "Why? Is he dying?"

Val's words ran together. "No. He heard I had two children and wanted to meet them. I introduced him to Greg and Jenny. I've met with him twice since. I wanted to tell you the last few times I saw you, but it wasn't the right time. What do you think?"

I didn't know how to respond. "Can I think about it? What about Eli?"

Val hastily added, "I hoped Eli could bring you."

"Let me talk to Eli. We'll let you know."

• • •

Eli spoke non-stop during the drive to meet our father, sucking his teeth every few minutes. "Why do we have to go today? I'm sure Donna needed me to pick up last-minute items for our Easter Sunday meal."

I gave him a side glance, shaking my head. "I spoke with your wife, and she has everything under control. So stop worrying. She wanted you to reconnect with Daddy before introducing him to your family in the summer." Eli and Donna were the proud parents of year-old twin boys.

Eli sucked his teeth for the hundredth time. "I don't know why I let you talk me into this. It's been ages since I last saw him. Even longer for you. He's a stranger to us."

I shrugged. "Yeah, but he's still our father."

And I miss him every day.

Eli chuckled. "Okay, smarty-pants." He added after a brief pause. "Hope Val shows up at the restaurant."

Val and my father were already seated, but he stood up when we arrived. I blinked. I always remembered him as a giant, but now Eli stood a couple of inches taller. I wracked my brains trying to think of the last time I saw my father. It seemed like yesterday when he'd lifted and held me in a tight embrace, letting me know how much he loved me. I had absolutely adored my father. I loved when sometimes his entire body shook whenever he enjoyed a good joke or when the sides of his mouth curled up and his eyes sparkled when he spoke to us. Did he remember me? Did he see me as the child he left or as a flawed person? My heart skipped a beat.

I hope he still loves me.

He started to say something then changed his mind. The years faded away with his hug. "Hi, kiddo. Good to see you."

I cast furtive glances at my father, wondering how the years had changed him, but he caught me in the act, giving me a beaming smile. The smile was gentle, yet it lit up his entire face with warmth and joy, inviting my smile. My eyes saw my Grandfather Joel, and my mind conjured up the face of my son. I turned toward Eli just in time to see the grin on his face. His eyes met mine before he proceeded to open the menu. He licked his lips. "Nice. Come to papa!" Everyone laughed and relaxed.

My father looked at me after we finished eating. "I'm so sorry, Nikki. Sorry that I wasn't there to welcome you. Do you remember how I always knew when you were sad or hurt? You look so sad. I'm sure you're carrying a heavy weight on your shoulders, and I'm sorry I wasn't around to relieve you of your burden. But do you know what? Even though I can't see the sparkle in your eyes, I know my beautiful princess is still in there. So try not to worry. Everything will work out fine. I missed you. I missed all of you."

CHAPTER TWENTY-THREE

I blinked a few times to keep the tears at bay.

Oh Daddy!

His gaze encompassed everyone. "I tried to contact your mother after I left, but she was so incensed that she wanted nothing to do with me. Because of her deep concern about public appearance, she disappeared before I could even provide financial support. I hope you can forgive me."

We nodded in unison.

My father sat up straighter. "It's been too long. I often wondered how your lives turned out. Val told me about her marriage and her children, whom I met. If you don't mind, Eli and Nikki, can you fill in the blank years for me?"

Eli looked at me. "We don't mind. I'm married with two children," he said, going on to talk about Donna, his twin boys, and his job.

All eyes turned toward me when Eli finished speaking. I froze like a deer in the headlights, blurting out what I thought to be safe words. "I have a job and my own place." Then my mind went blank before I started to wonder if he would be ashamed of me if he knew my secret. I didn't want to see the disappointment in his eyes.

Daddy's eyes opened wide, and his jaw dropped. "You're not living at home!" He shook his head. "I'm so sorry, Nikki. You're too young to be on your own."

Val stepped in. "It's okay, Daddy. She has a good place. We all know the owner, Mrs. Carmen. Mrs. Carmen treats her like a daughter. It's a safe place."

I mouthed a silent "Thank you" to Val and talked more about my apartment and my job. "What about you, Daddy?"

My father's eyes grew pensive. "Sometimes in life, we must know when enough is enough, move on, move out and take responsibility for our own happiness. I was miserable and drowning in the marriage, but I found a second chance at life with someone who respects me, supports me, and loves me. Her two boys welcomed my presence in their lives, since their mother raised them, without any support, after their father died. But pieces of my heart were missing—my own children were growing up without their father. I asked around until I found Val. Is it too late to be part of your lives? Can I get a second chance with you?"

After we gave him our wholehearted support, he continued. "When your mother disappeared and I couldn't find where you moved to, I decided to open bank accounts for all three of you, so you would have something in case anything happened to me." Then he handed each of us a bank book. We were too surprised to utter a word.

• • •

Later that evening, I sat at the desk to write a letter to Joel. That's when I knew I had made the right decision to meet with my father.

> My Dearest Joel,
>
> Happy fifth birthday!
>
> Where has the time gone? The first day of school must have been huge for you. My heart is bursting with pride. I still can't fathom that you're old enough to start school. Did you start the September when you turned four?
>
> Yet I'm sad. Sad that I didn't witness your joy, your wonder on that milestone. I hope you weren't scared or intimidated. I'm sorry I wasn't there for you. But I stand on the sidelines knowing that your parents rejoiced and supported you on that important day.
>
> On the topic of parents. I had lunch with my father today. I was eight years old when I last saw him. I thought he had forgotten about me or blamed me and my siblings for the breakup with our mother. I missed him every day. I grew up without him. His absence broke my heart. I couldn't share my joys or my pain with him. I felt abandoned. Alone. Did it affect my future? Probably. I would say definitely. That's why I desperately hope that you're growing up in a loving home.
>
> Just as I experience the pain of not having you in my life, I realize that it's also painful for my father, for some parents, to live with an absent child. There's always pain and longing, no matter the reason. Sometimes no matter how much we hurt, we must try to forgive ourselves and

those who hurt us so that we can move on in life. However-er, moving on and learning to forgive is a daily challenge. It's my fervent hope that someday you can forgive me. I also know that you will experience freedom when you forgive another person. Doing so, Joel, is the only way you can accept that your birth mother, that I, put you up for adoption, providing you with the hope of living your best life.

I know that act also affected you. Therefore, I start each day thinking of you and hoping that the way I live my life will somehow be a positive reflection in your life.

Although my father left, he continued to think about us, and eventually we reconnected. I'm happy just dreaming of connecting with you.

By the way, I think you'll look a bit like my father when you're older.

Always in my heart.

I reached for the shoebox stored under the desk and tucked in the letter at the back. For a few minutes, I silently gazed at the growing contents—my lifeline to my son.

CHAPTER
TWENTY-FOUR

"Fall in love with taking care of yourself. Fall in love with
the path of deep healing. Fall in love with becoming
the best version of yourself but with patience, with
compassion, and respect to your own journey."
—Sylvester McNutt

MY FATHER'S INNOCENT words woke me up—not from sleep that night, but from my sleepwalking through life. I had allowed my pain and grief to take over my life. Although my father saw the changes, he knew deep down that the child he knew still existed, and the love reflecting from his eyes assured me that his love remained unwavering.

As I gazed at the person in the mirror, I rested secure in the knowledge that Val, Eli, and Mrs. Carmen also loved me. But I asked the face staring back at me, "Do you love yourself?" No answer needed as I stared sightlessly into the past.

The face of my younger self materialized. "I thought I could find love in other people; I thought the world would end if I had no friends at school. I was young. I was mistaken."

The face of my older self appeared to respond. "We all make mistakes. We react to circumstances and situations based on our level of maturity. Isolated in a new school, I desperately wanted to belong. But I'm older now. I've paid the price. I'm paying the price. I know that nothing changes with laying blame. I can only look forward. I must learn to move on, to become someone who can lift her head, to stand up and dust herself off when she stumbles. At least, I must try."

My eyes focused. It was time to begin taking control of my life. Time to shake off the sand from my head that I'd buried in the sand. Time to find the light to help me love myself. I smiled, remembering how Mark Haynes left an impression on me the first time I met him at the non-academic classes.

Taking a page from Mark's book, I told the girl in the mirror, "They thought you were nobody. They made me believe I was nobody. But you, little Nikki Robinson, are somebody. True, I'm someone who's flawed and broken. Someone whose shoulders bear a heavy load. I'm sorry you thought the light of my love had grown as dim as when light is lowered in a lamp. I didn't mean to lose interest. But starting today, I believe I'm someone, and I'll do my best to love you. I'll love you so that my love will be greater for the people in my life, and it can spread to others."

I was grateful for my father's insight. I was still alive and realized I would go on making more mistakes. But I had already taken the first step to loving myself by getting away from my mother's negativity and her unrealistic expectation that I could go back to my previous life, that she could make me believe the lies she told herself. The princess within me wanted to be fully alive, and I made up my mind to let her not only feel the pain but also experience the joy in living. I wanted to smile through my tears.

I mused about my life in the Caribbean. I remembered screaming in delight as I jumped and skipped in the tropical rain, embracing everyone and every experience with an open heart and grins as wide and bright as the midday sun.

Now all I noticed were the clouds obscuring the sun, and the need to hide from life. I was aware that some things were beyond my control, but with my liquid sunshine within me, I could venture out in any weather, knowing the umbrella would shelter me from the rain while acknowledging the water served a useful purpose.

I raised my eyes above the mirror to figure out the semantics of my change. Yes—I'd endured a lot in my young life, but it taught me that I was stronger than I imagined and, as Mark reminded me, as flexible as elastic. Yes—I was not about to delude myself into thinking it would be a walk in the park when I stepped outside my comfort zone to learn something new or to meet new people. Yes—I know just trying to remove my camouflage would be like trying to remove the dirt from a landslide with a spoon. Yes—I would have to exercise patience for as long as it took.

I knew I couldn't change what had happened when I was fourteen, but I could start again with the hope of creating a different and better future. This day was the beginning of a new day for little Nikki Robinson. The light was sufficient for me to continue my journey along a new fork in the road.

My steps were lighter on my way to work, and it didn't cost me anything to paste a smile on my face. I was one step closer to becoming a better version of myself. But I had to fake it until I made it. Yet as the day progressed, it dawned on me that because I'd started concentrating on loving myself, I spent less time wallowing in my grief.

• • •

That evening, I strode confidently into the Bistro. "Hi, Mr. Benji! How was your day?" My eyes were alive and I was smiling from ear to ear.

He raised his head to look at me, his eyes wide. "Child, what did you eat?"

I laughed. "You're funny. I decided that it cost me nothing to have a change in attitude. What do you think?"

"I think you're onto something."

"What are we cooking this evening?"

"Curry chicken." He chuckled. "I still want to know what you ate."

I didn't want the evening to end.

The next day, I greeted my fellow cleaner. "Good morning, Marva," I said, giving her a sunny smile. "How are you this morning?"

Marva looked over her shoulder in surprise. In stunned silence, her eyes scanned me from head to toe. "Where is the other Nikki?"

"She has retired. I'm taking her place."

Marva laughed out loud. "I like the new Nikki." She eyed me again. "This is going to be interesting."

And it was. The change in my outlook caused a few eyebrows to raise at church, and people directed smiles my way when I sat closer to the front of the church. I still thought it prudent to avoid my mother and George. I wasn't about to tempt fate. Mrs. Carmen appeared at my side after the service. "Are you staying for fellowship?"

I nodded and smiled when she held my arm tightly, making it impossible for me to change my mind.

Light appeared as the cloud moved, allowing colour to come back into my world. In the following days, months, and years, my eyes no longer sought out the weeds along my way or followed the cracks in the sidewalks. They moved higher to admire the majesty of the ever-changing landscape in the different seasons, met the eyes of strangers, and marvelled at the beauty of the innumerable stars.

I compared my lifetime journey of loving myself to the journey along the roads in Dominica, where you were always climbing uphill and going downhill, but there were always stretches in between when you became totally exhilarated. That smooth expanse of road gave you permission to go faster, to feel the wind against your face, to be fully alive, to live in the moment. I hoped that someday the love would settle in my heart and allow me to coast on a smooth road of peace, security, and happiness.

CHAPTER
TWENTY-FIVE

"Resilience is accepting your new reality, even if it's less good than the one you had before. You can fight it, you can do nothing but scream about what you've lost, or you can accept that and try to put together something that's good."
—Elizabeth Edwards

IN THE FOLLOWING years, my life's journey continued uphill and downhill. The smooth expanse to coast remained elusive. I tried to get a firm foothold on the ever-shifting ground, but the hole in my heart remained empty, sometimes throwing me off balance. In addition, work consumed me to the extent that the passage of time felt different. One span of six months seemed like six years, while another felt like yesterday. I was not prepared for the suffering I faced, but I knew God was present and steady and always prepared to journey by my side. One scripture reading from church, John 16:32b, became an anchor for my life whenever the storms of life threatened to overwhelm me: "… *I am not alone, because the Father is with me.*"

Within five years, I earned a reputation as one of the best cleaners. The feedback was always positive:

"Always on time."

"Didn't waste precious minutes in idle chatter."

"Cleaned to perfection."

Work became my panacea.

One Friday afternoon toward the end of April, my boss called me to the office. She handed me a paper before remarking, "This is your next assignment. Residential cleaning. You start on Monday. A real estate agent wants this vacant house cleaned before it goes on the market. He asked for my best worker." She looked at me. "He said you can clean all his homes if he's happy with you." She stood up. "Good luck, Nikki."

"Thanks." I shoved the paper in my purse, intending to look at it the next day.

• • •

I left home early for my new assignment, pulling my hair back into a ponytail before taking the bus and a five-minute walk to the address. I had just reached the house when what appeared to be an expensive car—to my untrained eyes—pulled into the driveway. A slender man with short, auburn hair and about twenty years my senior got out and walked with a confident stride toward me.

He asked, "Nikki?" After I nodded, he continued. "I'm Julien. Julien Blaise." His hazel eyes with flecks of green appraised me. "I thought you would be older."

"Is that a problem?" I asked without a trace of a smile.

"No." His smile transformed the angles of his face into something gentle and magnetic. His warm voice put me at ease. "It's just that you're young to be one of their best workers."

I raised my eyebrows but kept silent. I didn't have to glance down at my crew-neck t-shirt to know I looked like a high school student.

"Come on in." He looked around before turning toward the front door. "The outside is a mess. No need to worry about it. I'll contract a lawn service to take care of it. Let's concentrate on the inside. There's a lot to be done."

It constantly amazed me that people lived in such conditions. The previous owners were the kind of people who thought it was a waste of money to fix broken appliances, used the floor as the garbage bin, and never bought a cleaning product during the ten years they owned the house. Grease, cigarette smoke, and dirt stained the walls, obscuring the original colour.

After we walked through the house, Julien turned to me. "Let me know what needs replacing. Can you get it cleaned and ready for showing in three weeks?"

"It's a lot of work in a short time. But manageable." My smile softened the words. "Let me look at the rooms again. Then I'll get the supplies and start cleaning tomorrow." I hesitated briefly. "Can you meet me at the office in the morning? I'll need transportation for the supplies."

"Of course. Not a problem. Let me know if you need anything else."

• • •

Meeting the deadline was a challenge, but I completed the cleaning in three weeks. The house sold soon after it went up for sale. When I reported back to my previous job, my boss gave me some documents informing me that, as promised, Julien kept his word by taking over my contract, since I'd demonstrated the high quality of work he wanted.

That assignment brought changes. No more commercial cleaning. Only residential cleaning. Because I spent long hours preparing the homes before Julien listed them, I reluctantly gave up my cleaning job at the Bistro but continued to help Mr. Benji in the kitchen whenever I had free time.

As my boss, Julien usually stopped off at the house at the end of the day or, if he wasn't busy, he made calls and conducted real estate business while I cleaned. The second house proved to be just as challenging as the first, but I worked like a Trojan to get it ready within the scheduled time. "I'm all done. The house is ready. You can list it."

Do I want to impress him?

Julien put aside his phone and looked at me. "I'm bushed! It was a long day." He stepped out of the kitchen, where he used the counter as a desk, to look around. "Well done, Nikki. I'm really pleased and happy with how you've transformed this place. How do you do it? You don't even look tired. As usual, you did an amazing job. I can't thank you enough." His sigh came out long and satisfied. "I don't know about you, but I'm also starving. Can we get a bite to eat?"

I hesitated "Ahh …" I was at a loss for words.

He's my boss.

I stalled. "Dinner?"

Can I trust him?

He laughed. "Yes, dinner. It was a long day and I'm sure you're hungry."

His smile, his laugh captivated me. My stomach flipped. "Yes."

CHAPTER TWENTY-FIVE

"Yes to dinner or yes you're hungry?"

I gave him a ghost of a smile and nervously replied. "Yes to both." I looked for my purse in an attempt to cover my nervousness.

• • •

Julien sat back after we finished the Italian dinner. "That was good. Wasn't it?"

"Yes. Thank you for dinner." I sighed with relief that my hands hadn't shaken while I ate.

Julien took a sip of his coffee. "Would you like anything else? Dessert?"

"I'm good, but thank you."

He rested the cup on the table. "You don't talk much, do you? I like that about you. You put all your energy into your work." He continued, not expecting a response. "It's late. Can I drop you home?"

"Yes, thanks."

How thoughtful!

Over the next months, I relaxed in Julien's presence and began to trust him. Without a conscious thought, I started to look forward to his company. Although I packed a sandwich, snacks, and a drink, he also brought me different lunches—sometimes a Greek salad, fish and chips, or a chicken meal. Julien did the necessary heavy lifting, making my work easier, and always provided dinner at the end of each job. The dinner became a celebration—a celebration that sometimes lasted for hours.

I was honest enough to admit that I liked Julien. My heart pounded when it dawned on me that what I felt for Julien was different from the way I felt about my family. I remembered that when I was about ten years old, I had snuck into the kitchen to take a gulp of rum, on a dare. It was difficult to find the words to describe the initial feelings. It was a combination of exhilaration and euphoria with a lowered inhibition thrown in. My feelings for Julien were the same, yet different. I wanted those indescribable feelings to continue.

One morning I spoke to my reflection in the small bathroom mirror in the apartment. "Lord, I must decide whether I should keep my broken heart all wrapped up and safely tucked away in the darkness or let in the light and take a chance at life. I'm a good person. A good person who just made the wrong choice. But how long do I have to bear the punishment for my sin?

I've learned my lesson. I just want to know what it's like to be happy. Sure, I'm still vulnerable, but I've learned that there are no guarantees in this life. I want to see what a relationship, a true relationship, is like. I may be inexperienced, but I know Julien is interested in me. Sure, he's older, but he's nothing like the boys at school. In fact, our age difference brings me comfort and peace. I think it's time. Time to take a chance at joy and love. Time to find joy in the face of my grief."

CHAPTER
TWENTY-SIX

"You may not control all the events that happen to you,
but you can decide not to be reduced by them."
—Maya Angelou

JULIEN BLAISE DECLARED his intentions during dinner a few evenings later. I thought I was ready, but I panicked when faced with reality. I almost choked on my food in my haste to inform him that I had no time to date and that I saw my sister, my brother, and their families regularly, my father occasionally, and my mother on her birthday and at Christmas.

Julien simply smiled at me. "I understand. No pressure."

"Thanks. Ahh ... can I ask you a question?" I sat up straighter.

No pressure.

"Sure. Anything."

"Have you ever made a decision that you regretted?"

He laughed dryly. "At the risk of sounding trite, I would say my marriage."

"Sorry."

"It's okay. It's water under the bridge. But it taught me that I should always listen to my heart and do what's right instead of worrying about social expectations and thinking of myself as a failure if I didn't try to make it work." He paused before continuing. "Now I want to be a better person—do better, be better." He looked directly into my eyes. "I want us to be more than friends, but I'll let you set the pace. Is that okay with you?"

I nodded, letting my muscles relax.

During our following conversations, Julien talked about his love for the real estate business and his children. His youngest lived with his mother, and his daughter and another son lived on their own.

• • •

Julien patiently waited for me to be comfortable enough to talk about my life. I elaborated on the easy part—my love for the island and how it provided security and happiness until I turned thirteen. It took me longer to give him a summary of my years after migrating to Canada because I first had to accept responsibility for the choice I made in high school and somehow deal with my pain. The telling became important, since he didn't need to know all the details.

I lost my first love, my son, and romantic love was the furthest thing on my mind. I wasn't looking for it, but I wanted it. Yet I was hesitant. Not afraid, just hesitant. I hoped that wanting this love wouldn't end up the same way as when I desperately needed a friend in high school. But I knew that I could trust Julien. Trust was enough. Enough for love to find me. Julien persisted. He invited me to dinners and events to meet his friends, but only if I didn't object.

I called Val after meeting his friends. "I'd like you and Dad to meet Julien."

"Sure. We'd love to meet him."

"Thanks." I paused briefly. "Ahh … I told you he's older than me."

"And …"

"I think he's about twenty years older. Do you think he's too old for me?"

"What do you think? Forget age for a minute. Does he have qualities you like?"

"Yes."

"If dating Julien makes you happy, then do so."

• • •

Julien and I drove to Toronto soon after my conversation with Val. We had a relaxing lunch with my dad, Val, and her family. The expected barrage of questions from Val and my father didn't materialize. I puffed up with pride knowing that Julien held his own.

Of course. He's experienced!

Did that mean they approved? Did that mean they liked him?

Afterwards Julien remarked, "This soup is delicious," referring to Val's Caribbean version of a pea soup. He continued. "Thank you for the meat pie. It tasted similar to the tourtière my mother made."

Val turned to him in a conspiratorial voice. "I'm glad you enjoyed the pie." Her voice dropped even lower. "I make meat pies regularly but added a special blend of spices just for you ... and I used pork, beef, and veal" She turned and smiled at me. "Nikki is also getting to be a good cook."

We spent the next hour discussing different topics, including cultural foods and real estate. Somehow, Val got in a few personal questions, which Julien managed expertly. Then the muscles in my shoulders tensed and my breathing became shallow when I thought my father was going to ask the dreaded question: "Son, what's your intention?" My mind was so wrapped up in that one question that I missed the end of the conversation. It must have ended well because there were smiles and hugs when we left.

Julien made me smile on our way home when he observed, "I like your family. Your sister and father are very protective of you. I understand." He held the steering wheel with one hand and held my hand with the other. "I cherish you. I'll protect you with my life. I won't let anything happen to you."

I smiled tenderly. My heart sang.

That feels good!

"Now, I'm looking forward to meeting your brother. Does he enjoy a satisfying meal too?"

"Does he ever!"

"I can't wait!"

• • •

A week later, Eli certainly amazed Julien when we had dinner with him and Donna at a steak and seafood restaurant in Kitchener. Eli's hard stare lasted a few minutes. "So. You're dating my sister."

Julien nodded, giving Eli one of his captivating smiles.

Eli took a step closer and spoke to Julien in a whisper, loud enough for me to hear. "She's special. Treat her well or you'll answer to me."

Julien didn't appear intimidated by Eli's size. "Always." He placed a hand on Eli's shoulder, disarming him.

Satisfied, Eli nodded and smiled. After we took our seats, he turned his attention to the menu and grinned. "I've died and gone to Heaven."

After dinner, Julien whispered, "Your brother really loves his food. He needs a lot of fuel to sustain his size." He laughed. "I like him. And Donna. Did I tell you I'm meeting Eli to play golf?"

• • •

Julien taught me a lot about the real estate industry, listening when I courageously made practical suggestions or talked to him about my ideas for making improvements to increase the value of a house.

We also had fun going to shows in Toronto and in Stratford and taking a few day trips to places like Niagara Falls, Niagara-on-the-Lake, Elora Gorge, the Bruce Peninsula National Park, and the neighbouring communities. While I enjoyed walking and hiking with Julien, I decided that I wasn't a suitable partner for sports like baseball and golf.

Although we frequented the neighbourhood restaurants, I was more relaxed in Julien's kitchen. Preparing meals in the spacious kitchen reminded me of the kitchen at the Bistro, and it gave me an opportunity to impress Julien with my cooking skills. I loved the ranch-style house with a beautiful landscape and lots of windows in one of the older neighbourhoods and close to the Waterloo Park. As a lesson in real estate, Julien explained how he had been in the perfect position to buy the property when the market was down.

• • •

Julien introduced me to his children when he invited them to lunch at his favourite restaurant. Their gaze moved from their father to me, then back to their father, before they settled into chairs away from me.

His daughter asked, "And who is this?" as she looked down her nose at me.

Julien looked at me and smiled. "This is Nikki. When I invited the three of you, I mentioned I wanted you to meet someone important to me." He reached out to hold my hand.

I only heard plates clattering and the murmur of the other patrons.

Julien's eyes widened. He raised his eyebrows while his children stared back at him with expressionless faces. "Do you have a problem with me dating Nikki?"

His daughter appeared to be the spokesperson. "We thought you meant someone from work. You know, a work thing."

Julien's eyes blazed. "I don't see how you came to that conclusion. But listen to me. Listen to me very carefully. If I hear any one of you disrespect Nikki, you will answer to me. Do I make myself clear?"

They grumbled, "Yeah. Sure. Can we eat now?"

After a silent meal, they threw a goodbye to their father but ignored me. Julien reached for my hand. "I love my children, but they are spoiled brats. I'm sorry."

I squeezed his hand.

"Luckily, they were older when we divorced, but their mother and I struggled with our co-parenting duties. One reason is that their mother continues to speak negatively about me, thus forcing them to take sides. They see you as competition for the time they have with me."

"I understand."

Is that what it is?

"I'm sorry again. You don't have to worry about going through something like this a second time."

CHAPTER

TWENTY-SEVEN

"We delight in the beauty of the butterfly, but rarely admit
the changes it has gone through to achieve that beauty."
—Maya Angelou

I TRUSTED THAT Julien would always provide a buffer against his children's
hostility. I didn't have to put on airs or work to impress Julien. He didn't
put me in a mould of the type of person he wanted for a wife. I enjoyed his
company, and he made me happy. My confidence blossomed. It was like
a rosebud that thrived, opening to display its glorious colour with proper
grooming and care. He liked me the way I was and that was enough. I was
enough. We left the office early one Friday afternoon for a surprise picnic in
the Waterloo Park.

Luckily, the weather cooperated with the sunshine and higher-than-nor-
mal temperature for mid-May. We didn't need the blankets, so we used them
to cover the bench in the gazebo. It was my first visit to the park, and even
though I wanted to peek into the picnic basket, I stood, lifting my face to
enjoy the fresh air before letting my eyes roam around to feast on the beauty
of nature. When I heard Julien clear his throat, I turned, my eyes zeroing in
on the basket, happily anticipating lunch. Then, from the corner of my eye,
I saw Julien holding a ring box toward me. I took a step back as an involuntary gasp escaped before my hand could muffle the sound.

Julien smiled. "Nikki, you bring joy and happiness to my life. I love your
delightful laughter and the sparkle in your eyes when you're happy, and I

admire your generous nature. You're my partner at work, and I can't imagine my life without you. I love you, Nikki. Will you be my partner in life? Will you marry me?"

The beat of my heart raced. My hand went to my chest in a vain attempt to keep my heart from jumping out. A wave of emotions flooded my mind. Excitement. Joy. Happiness. They left me giddy. It was as if I had taken too big a sip from a glass of rum. I was still standing, although a bit rocky on my feet.

My smile matched the brilliance of the afternoon sun. "Yes. I will."

Julien slipped the ring on my finger as a single butterfly fluttered around us. I mentally joined the butterfly in its dance.

• • •

The happy haze lasted through dinner, but doubts assailed me later that evening. I phoned Val for reassurance and advice.

"Is it too soon?"

"Do you love him?"

I answered honestly. "I don't know." I sighed heavily. "I don't know how I should feel. I do know I feel safe with him. I trust him. I trust him with my life. I'm never afraid to speak up, to express myself when I'm with him."

"Nikki, honey, I'll support you no matter what you decide. You deserve happiness. Vivian Greene, a motivational speaker and author, said, 'Life isn't about waiting for the storm to pass … It's about learning to dance in the rain.' You're still going through your storm. Dance, my sister, dance."

"It's fun to dance in the rain."

"Exactly! Didn't you say a butterfly appeared after you accepted Julien's proposal?"

"Yes. A beautiful one."

"Do you know what butterflies symbolize?"

"No."

"A fresh start. A change."

"Really! That sounds about right. I'm ready for a fresh start."

She chuckled. "Then I would say you've made the right decision." I could hear Val's hesitation. "Will you be okay telling Mama?"

"Yes," I said, although I was not looking forward to doing so.

• • •

I could only summon enough courage to phone my mother a month before the wedding date. If I were a drinker, I probably would have gulped down a few glasses of my favourite wine for fortification. Instead, I took a deep breath and blurted out my invitation.

My mother listened until I finished speaking. "Really, Nikki? I'm your mother, and you waited until the last minute to let me know you're getting married? I knew it! I knew you don't love me."

Lord, give me strength.

Her voice rose an octave. "I'm your mother, for crying out loud. Don't you think that as your mother I should at least meet the man you're marrying? What kind of man is he? How do I know he's the right man for you?" I closed my eyes and took a deep breath in time to hear the rest of the conversation. "I bet I'm the last to hear the news."

I kept silent, letting her rant and rave for a few more minutes. "I hope you can make it."

"Well, I'll try. I hope your father isn't invited. Does the last-minute invitation extend to George?"

I raised my eyes upward, ignoring the comment about my father. "Yes. The invitation includes George."

Marian responded grudgingly. "All right. I'm sure George will want to go." She paused dramatically. "At least now you can start having children."

I hung up.

CHAPTER
TWENTY-EIGHT

"The way I see it, if you want the rainbow,
you gotta put up with the rain."
—Dolly Parton

TWO MONTHS AFTER my twenty-sixth birthday, I sat at a hotel dressing table staring blindly into the mirror. After a few minutes, I closed my eyes to return to another place and time. To the island where I strolled barefoot along my favourite beach, with the waves gently lapping against my legs, and black sand oozing between my toes. My cares and worries were forgotten as I lifted my face to the warm sun, enjoying the caress of the salty sea breeze.

The image popped like a balloon and vanished when Val burst through the door without knocking. "Nikki, honey, I'm so sorry. I saw Mama leaving your room and I knew from her expression that she was up to no good. What did she say?"

I looked at my sister in the mirror. Back to the real world inhabited by my mother. My eyes reflected pain and were full of unshed tears. "She said that I should be happy someone wanted to marry me because I'm damaged goods."

"Damaged goods? Lord, give me strength. Ignore her." She leaned over and wrapped her arms around my neck.

I closed my eyes, but my heart broke.

How can I?

My blanket of grief had lightened and returned to a shawl of grief when I met Julien and eventually became his fiancée. I had intentionally assigned my pain and grief to the back of my mind. My confidence was at an all-time high. But my mother's words brought my grief and pain back to the front. She eroded my confidence.

Why? Why use those words?

I sighed heavily. It's like those words wove their way and assumed permanent residence with my grief.

My sister's eyes met mine in the mirror. "I know the problem. She's bored. That's what happens when you retire early to please someone else. I had suggested that she continue working fewer hours in the hospital kitchen, but did she listen to me? Of course not. It's what George wanted. Now she has too much time on her hands."

"Yeah. Time to find the right words to belittle me."

"I'm so sorry, Nikki. She gets a thrill picking on you. I think it's because she knows you won't respond." She sighed. "But don't let her spoil your big day." She grinned before continuing. "Wait till she sees Daddy. She'll have a fit. That will give her a taste of her own medicine." Val paused. "We love you and we want you to be happy," she continued, tightening her hug. "Now, let me look at you."

I turned around and stood up.

Val stepped closer to me and slid her arm around my waist. "You look beautiful!"

I fluffed my permed hair, styled in a medium-length bob, before using my hand to emphasize how the white, mid-length dress hugged my trim figure. I rested my head on Val's arm for a brief minute, took a deep breath, and smiled. "I'm ready."

But my mother's words still lingered in my mind as I left the room. From the depth of my soul, I asked God to make me a fitting wife when, minutes later, I exchanged vows with forty-five-year-old Julien Blaise before our family and friends in a simple ceremony at a hotel south of the city.

Julien's children accepted the wedding invitation, wanting to remain in their father's favour. Nevertheless, they made a statement by wearing all black to our wedding. After the ceremony, they waited until their father left my side to engage in a discussion with a few of his golfing buddies before they pounced on me. In a split second, they pulled up chairs to surround me. "Don't think we don't know what you're up to."

"What?" Their unexpected appearance made my heartbeat gallop.

"Don't play the innocent with us. You can't fool us with your virginal act. You're young enough to be his daughter. Couldn't you find someone your age?" The barrage of accusations continued for minutes while I sat silent, defenceless and in shock.

Finally, I found my voice. "I think you'd better leave. All of you."

They stood up in one accord. "We will. But we'll be watching you."

A few minutes later, Val approached. "What was that all about?"

I gave a dry laugh. "Among other things, his children thought it best to let me know that the house was a surprise gift for their mother, but their parents divorced before he told her about it. They think the house rightfully belongs to her and I would have to vacate if anything happened to their father. Oh yes. They stressed that they would not set foot in the house because I lived there, and I wasn't welcome at their homes."

Val took a step back. "Wow! They don't waste time. Did they say anything else?"

"That I was a gold-digger, using their father's money, their money, to go places, suggesting that I enjoy the ride while I could because it would end one day."

Val put an arm around my shoulder. "Never mind them. They don't know you. We'll continue this discussion another day. This is your day. I just want you to relax, enjoy it, and be happy. Okay?"

I leaned into Val. "Okay."

"Did you get a chance to notice our mother?"

"Not if I can help it."

Val chuckled. "You haven't missed much." At my shrug, she continued. "Too bad she can't be happy for you."

"That's because she thinks she can just erase what happened."

"I know. You are your own person now. You're walking your own path."

"Would I be considered a bad daughter if I avoided her as much as possible?"

"No, honey. I think that would be a wise decision." She paused. "Hey! You know what they say!"

"What?" I rolled my eyes. "Who said what?" My sister was a fan of the American show *Jeopardy*, remembering bits of trivia from the show, finding her own clues and answers, and driving us crazy in the process.

"Okay. It's really Henry Wadsworth Longfellow who said that 'Into each life some rain must fall.'"

I shook my head, but the laughter bubbled up and I grinned. "Valerie, I won't let them rain on my parade."

We burst out laughing.

CHAPTER
TWENTY-NINE

"I will welcome happiness for it enlarges my heart; Yet I
will endure sadness for it opens my soul. I will acknowledge rewards for they are my due; Yet I will welcome
obstacles for they are my challenge."
—Og Mandino

BOTH JULIEN AND I brought different expectations to the marriage. Julien's divorce years earlier had left him bitter and distrustful. He often told me he trusted me, and he found it relaxing to be with me without getting into arguments and fights. After that, I made sure my husband got his wish. I didn't want to be seen in a negative light.

I concentrated on my new role as a wife but remained uncertain as to what it all meant. I also didn't want my husband to know that he married someone who was, according to my mother, damaged. That part of my life would remain my secret, but I would do my best to please him, to reciprocate his love. I made a conscious decision to be happy. It was effortless to display my affection, and I appreciated all the little moments of joy, accepting the love that came into my life with all my heart.

Julien gave me a place I called home. A place where I belonged. Because I wanted the atmosphere in our home to be different from when I lived with my mother, I made sure to praise and compliment Julien, avoided unnecessary arguments as much as possible. I continued to support him in his work and expressed my appreciation and gratitude with a smile and an embrace, always letting him know how I felt.

I admired the fact that Julien was always in tune with himself. He was independent and didn't rely on me to make him happy. He respected my space and boundaries, thus allowing me to do the same, increasing my trust in him. He gave me space to grow into my own, and space to be with family and friends separately, and together we supported each other. This brought us more intimacy and passion and a greater commitment to our marriage. When I joked that he had maturity, he responded with a laugh. "It comes with age."

Although I was the junior partner in our business, Julien discussed all real estate matters with me. Outside of work, he didn't hesitate to talk about his emotions, his desires, his mistakes, and what he would like to see for our future. I married someone I could depend on, someone who kept his word.

Contrary to what his children thought, I didn't marry Julien for his money. One evening while relaxing with a glass of wine and enjoying the sunset, Julien cleared his throat. "Looking after the household must be a change for you."

"A big change."

"Can we spend some time talking about the household budget?"

"Sure."

"Good. I also want to set aside an emergency fund and open a spousal RRSP for you. We're in different places in our lives, so it's important to make time over the next few weeks so you can educate yourself financially and I can discuss my financial status fully with you."

• • •

The drawback of living with a secret and lies was that I functioned on two levels. On one hand, I functioned well within my marriage, thriving and maturing as an individual, but on the other hand, I relied on medications to make me appear normal, to keep painful memories away, and to dull my grief.

My shoulder-length hair became brittle, forcing the hairdresser to cut it short in layers so that it would have more volume. In addition, I developed diarrhea and became sensitive to light, sound, and smell.

I hope he assumes it's because I'm a newlywed.

CHAPTER TWENTY-NINE

Luckily, my husband didn't pry. He wasn't worried, since I controlled those issues with medication.

• • •

Because I didn't have role models around me, I found out the hard way that both parties in a marriage required patience and endurance to build a lasting relationship. Getting through holidays during the first year required adjustment, compromise, and change. Julien took his children to a restaurant on their birthdays, and we spent Thanksgiving Sunday with my family, leaving the next day free to spend it as we wished. Christmas became the sticky point.

I wanted to spend the day with Julien. Julien wanted to see his children. Val suggested we have lunch with Julien's family and dinner with my family. We went back and forth with different options, but nothing worked for us. In the end, I reluctantly agreed that Julien would spend Christmas Day with his children. I would face my family alone. How would my family view this pragmatic compromise? I wasn't looking forward to finding out.

How can I avoid my mother and George?

I knew it was uncharitable, but I prayed that George would fall on the ice, or they would both be sick with the flu. Anything.

My prayer remained unanswered when my mother and George walked into Val's living room. I steeled myself for my mother's sarcastic remarks. "Where's your husband?" She looked around. "Is he here?"

My eyes pleaded with Val, who responded. "No, Mama. Julien is spending Christmas with his children. Nikki came with Eli and Donna." She held out a hand to indicate the way to the kitchen. "Why don't you come with me. You should get a drink."

Marian ignored Val. "Hmmm. Is there trouble in paradise already?" Her eyes sparkled as if she had just received an amazing gift. Taking a step closer to the centre of the room, she turned on her preachy voice. "If you ask me, I think you got married too quickly."

I cleared my throat. "No one asked you."

She glared at me for daring to interrupt. "What kind of man misses the first Christmas with his wife's family?" She smirked. "What did you—"

Val stepped in front of her, effectively cutting her off. "Enough, Mama. Let's go to the kitchen. You definitely need a drink," she said, glaring at George, who appeared unconcerned.

I pulled my shawl of grief tighter around me and hung my head to avoid pitiful glances. Shame and embarrassment rose up like a wall to surround me. I didn't like my mother. I sighed deeply.

Next time, I'll hide in the bathroom.

CHAPTER
THIRTY

"She stood in the storm and when the wind did not blow
her way, she adjusted her sails."
—Elizabeth Edwards

ADJUSTMENTS AND COMPROMISES. I made them to avoid confrontation. I made them to keep living my best life. Living my best life with family and friends—friends who I later discovered played a key role within a marriage. I'd met two couples—Stella and her husband, Roger, and Jasmine and her husband, Ken, when Julien courted me. Over the years, Julien took a break from marital responsibilities to spend time with the men, and as couples we took holidays together and attended some social events.

I also allowed Julien's friends the space to maintain their friendship with him. As his wife, I learned to socialize with them. It was easy. Besides giving Julien time alone with them, I let them do most of the talking whenever I was in their company. They talked constantly about their married children and grandchildren, complete with 101 pictures. I was an outsider.

I don't belong to that club.

I had just left the room during one of our early social gatherings and unintentionally eavesdropped on their conversation. Stella, who always spoke her mind and about who everyone said had no filter, spoke to Julien in a loud voice, not caring that her words carried.

"We were wondering," Jasmine said, "you already have three children. Any plans for more?" I edged closer to the door but didn't hear Julien's response. When I returned to the group, I had to endure looking at the numerous pictures of their grandchildren.

Therefore, Julien's question one Sunday morning didn't take me by surprise. "Would you like to have a child?"

My heart began to beat faster, although I had my answer ready. I had hoped and prayed this day would never come. "I hadn't thought about it." I paused to find the right words. "You already have three children and one grandchild. Are you okay with not having one with me?"

"Are you sure?"

I gave him a bright smile. "I'm sure."

He let out a huge exhalation of pent-up breath. "That's fine with me too. You're the best, Nikki!"

My heart rate slowed as I plastered on a false smile. How could I replace my absent child? His memory remained as fresh as on the day I birthed him. I hadn't even experienced the joy in holding my baby. How could I have more children?

The hole is still in my heart.

The conversation with Julien made me think about my delivery and the promise I made to myself that day. Therefore, months later, I gave Val the same answer when she diplomatically brought up the subject of more children.

Nevertheless, Marian saw things differently. She waited three years into the marriage before confronting me. "When are you going to have a child? Why are you waiting? I know you can have children."

• • •

I also adjusted at work. I enjoyed working with Julien, and he agreed with my suggestion to decorate one house. Home staging was a relatively new concept reserved for luxury properties, but since Julien's niche included homes that needed a lot of work inside and outside the property, I reasoned that adding furnishings and accents would get the property noticed faster. After our gamble paid off, Julien gladly gave me free reign to decorate all his homes.

Over the years, I continued to decorate Julien's properties for sale, buying a couple of the artworks at the Art Gallery Kitchener. The gallery displayed contemporary visual art, including local, national, Indigenous, and international works. Julien personally owned several pieces from the gallery and introduced me to the manager, Gavin Alleyne, as a close acquaintance.

I always chatted with Gavin and bonded with his wife and daughter. Gavin was born in Ontario to Caribbean parents but moved to New York at an early age and later attended Columbia University in Manhattan. It was there that he met an African-American, Carissa, who later became his wife when they moved to Montreal to begin their life together. As a prominent photographer, Gavin started a children's photography club and opened a photography studio. He and Carissa also ran an art gallery there before the family of three moved to the Waterloo region after the couple accepted an offer to manage the art gallery.

CHAPTER
THIRTY-ONE

"The oak fought the wind and was broken,
the willow bent when it must and survived."
—Robert Jordan, *The Fires of Heaven*

I ADJUSTED AND matured as I learned to deal with different people and to make decisions as a wife and business associate. In addition, my marriage to Julien gave me the opportunity to know the new me—my likes and dislikes, my strengths and my weaknesses. However, I chose not to think about my secret or dwell on my grief and failures. I relegated them to the back of my mind as I concentrated on building a new life. I learned to be grateful for the little things—for the people in my life, for my marriage, and for the opportunity to work in a different field. Although we didn't attend a church, I was at peace knowing we lived a good life.

I worked hard to learn as much as I could from Julien. He was patient with my inexperience and generous with his finances. When he encouraged me to learn new things and try different activities during our down time, I chose to volunteer at a dog rescue facility dedicated to rescuing, rehabilitating, and re-homing stray, abandoned, and surrendered dogs.

• • •

My life continued to change, but the abiding love for my son remained constant. I continued to celebrate Joel's birthdays in private. The location of the celebration depended on the unpredictable March weather. Sometimes

I sat in my car in a park, a surprise gift from Julien after receiving my driver's licence, with a slice of cake and cup of tea, then took a stroll to enjoy the sun. On rainy days, I stayed in a café, or I baked a cake at home if the day called for icy weather.

Although Joel remained a secret, thoughts of him were always front and centre in my mind. Writing made me feel closer to him. Writing helped eased the pain in my heart.

My Dearest Joel,

Happy birthdays! Happy everything!

You've had many memorable events, celebrations, and birthdays. How I wished that I could have celebrated them with you. Did you celebrate with siblings? And with friends? I remember wanting desperately to have a friend in high school. But I also remember one friend, Mark, who stood by me, encouraged me, and made me smile. Friends are important in every phase of your life. Celebrate with them. Celebrate them.

I also wish that I were around to support and help you navigate the major life changes. I know that teenage years can be challenging. I remember how I longed to be a teenager. Bullying, bad choices, and regret filled my teenage years. These were painful years. I hope your teenage years were much different from mine. I pray that you sailed through yours. They are emotional years, and I hope you enjoyed yours.

Personal relationships were not part of my teenage years. I hope they are in yours. I'm sure you experienced puppy love in middle school. Now you're a teenager and probably dating someone in your class. I hope your first serious girlfriend doesn't break your heart.

This is your coming-of-age journey. You're growing up, and I know that growing up isn't easy. It's the time when you'll go through personal growth, a time when you'll see the world differently, form your own opinions, and make choices that can impact the rest of your life. Yet I hope you can still find joy and wonder.

Prom night. I didn't have a prom night. There was no reason to celebrate and no one to celebrate it with. I don't think my mother even mentioned it. Hope you enjoyed yours. I've heard that it's the biggest night of a child's high school years. I'm sure you'll always remember yours. Did you ask a girl to the prom? Did you rent a limo?

Congratulations, my dear Joel, on all your accomplishments!

I do hope you go to college or university. Are you going to an institution close to home, or do you have to leave home? Learn as much as you can. A good education will allow you to have more options in life and more career opportunities. I know you'll make a wise decision.

I pray every day that your environment provides structure and stability, that you find time to engage in activities you enjoy, and that you treat others the way you would want to be treated.

So sorry I couldn't be there for you, but I've celebrated and I'm celebrating all you have achieved. I hope you're happy and thriving.

Always in my heart.

● ● ●

I continued to turn to Val for advice. During one of her visits, she held my hands. "Nikki, I know you worked hard to get where you are. I'm proud of your success."

"Thanks, Val." I smiled.

"Did Julien's children change their minds?"

"About?"

"Visiting you."

"No."

Val sighed. "I've thought a lot about your situation. I could only think of one thing that would solve your problem." She paused briefly at my raised eyebrows. "That's finding a way to build your own nest egg."

CHAPTER THIRTY-ONE

"How? I work long hours now. Getting a second job is out of the question."

"I know it's hard. But the nest egg will be yours and yours alone. You need to be financially secure, because if anything happens to Julien, his children will fight tooth and nail to make sure you get nothing."

I nodded in agreement.

"In fact, I bet they'll kick you out of the house the very next day."

It was a challenge to figure out how I could secure financial means not tied to my marriage. Weren't the funds of a second job also considered marital assets? I thought of asking Mrs. Carmen but decided to try praying about it first. I knew she would recommend prayer.

Although I no longer helped Mr. Benji in the Bistro's kitchen, Mrs. Carmen remained my surrogate mother. My light. After my marriage, Julien and I enjoyed the occasional Saturday brunch, but Mrs. Carmen and I had lunch at the Bistro on the last Friday of every month. Just the two of us. It gave me an opportunity to celebrate, to share, to get advice, to catch up, or to simply enjoy her company.

I released my anxiety and stress, believing Mrs. Carmen when she said that prayers do work. A week later, I came across a regional listing for a small three-bedroom bungalow that had been on the market for six months. It was in terrible condition, and no one had made an appointment to view it. It needed major repairs, updates, and a lot of tender loving care. During the brief time on the market, it had three significant price drops. Still no offers. The sellers grew desperate. It was the answer to my prayer. When I explained to Julien that I wanted financial security in case anything happened to him, he readily agreed to the purchase, putting the title in my name.

Over the next ten months, I spent every available moment at the property in Waterloo and every penny I had to renovate it. I helped demolish the interior and helped with the tiling, the laying of the floors, and the painting. I lost more than half of the back yard when I added an all-season sunroom that opened out on a large deck, but the addition made up for the loss. Besides, the landscape company gave the exterior a striking makeover. Then I rented the furnished property to a bank manager, who didn't hesitate to pay the high rent.

CHAPTER
THIRTY-TWO

"The direction you choose to face determines whether
you're standing at the end or the beginning of a road."
—Richelle E. Goodrich

JULIEN AND I continued to live the life that suited us. A life of learning and growing, of compromises and adjustments. I refilled my prescription whenever I noticed hair in the sink or my skin started to itch, and I frequently sported two-strand twists, ponytails, or braids hairstyles to cover any noticeable patches. Therefore, when Julien began to feel sick, he played down his illness, blaming his tiredness and loss of appetite on our hectic work schedule. Finally, I forced him to seek medical attention when he started to lose weight.

The laboratory and imaging tests showed that Julien had cirrhosis, severe liver damage caused by a genetic digestive disorder known as Alagille syndrome. He took the recommended medications but continued to drink alcohol with his friends after visiting and eating out with his children.

The muscles in my shoulders automatically bunched up and my heart sank when he returned from those visits. I fretted. I threatened. I begged Julien to stop drinking, but he simply laughed and waved aside my concerns. He believed that taking the medication without a lifestyle change was enough to return him to perfect health. I wanted him to change his habits. He ignored my attempts. My inexperience worked against me.

Am I a bad wife?

I had a distant memory of women on the island talking about their husbands when they thought that we, the children, couldn't hear. Now their words made sense: "What do you expect me to do? He's a grown man." I remained powerless.

• • •

Months later, I couldn't remember what I was doing when the ambulance took Julien to the hospital. The sinking feeling in my chest spread over my body, and fear and uncertainty crept into my mind. I drove to the hospital in a daze. The diagnosis confirmed my worst fears. Not only had Julien's liver function worsened, but he'd also developed other complications.

When his liver couldn't make enough of certain blood proteins, the pressure in the veins caused fluid to accumulate in his legs, feet, and ankles. Then he got a stabbing pain in his right upper abdomen just under his ribs, which the doctor said happened because of fluid retention and enlargement of his spleen and liver caused by the cirrhosis. I prayed there would be no more unwelcome news.

How much more can I bear?

More than I thought. I sat at the edge of the office chair, gripping my hands tightly when the doctor told me that Julien had developed jaundice. My heart jolted then dropped like a stone. My shoulders slumped. The doctor explained that Julien's diseased liver was unable to remove enough of the blood waste product from his blood. Julien had a yellowing of the skin and the whites of the eyes, and his urine had turned dark. The doctor explained that the toxins also built up in Julien's brain, causing mental confusion, and it became difficult for him to concentrate, leading him to experience personality changes.

At times I convinced myself that Julien would get better, that he would bounce back. Maybe he'd prove the doctors wrong. Maybe I could share a laugh with my husband again. But these changes startled me, reminding me of the reality—Julien was dying.

My heart grew numb with pain. Sometimes my anger spilled over. When that happened, I stayed away from the hospital until I had my emotions under control. I was angry at myself for not being a better wife. What wife allowed her husband to get sick because of a lifestyle choice? I was angry at Julien for getting sick. Didn't he know I needed him? What would I do without him? The emptiness at home brought back the darkness and the loneliness—the loneliness I had experienced in the delivery room and the darkness that followed. I didn't want to go through another loss. Would I survive this time? Would the grief crush me?

My grief hadn't crushed me in high school because I had accepted support from Mark Haynes. I wanted to survive. I vowed to survive.

I'm strong. I'm elastic.

I popped pills to control my dermatological conditions. I started wearing a wig again. I gladly let Donna and Eli shop, prepare light meals, and take care of our home. Mrs. Carmen provided soups, and my sister offered support every night and kept my parents apprised of the situation.

After my internal struggle, it became easier to present Julien with a happy face. He spoke earnestly to me during one of his lucid moments. "Nikki, you're still young. You have a lot to offer. If the worst happens, I want you to get married again. I want you to be happy."

I choked. I allowed the silent tears to stream down my face.

Don't leave me!

My sadness became overwhelming.

How am I ever going to survive without you?

But in my heart, I knew it was hard to ask him to stay when his body had started to break down, when he was in intense pain.

Julien also apologized for the trouble his children might cause after he was no longer around to protect me. "It was a smart move, buying that house. It's all yours. It's a place no one can take from you. Spend as much money as you need to improve it."

Oh, my love!

My heart broke. Although I wasn't ready to say goodbye, I had no choice. I had to let him go. I had to enter the waiting period. Waiting for the inevitable.

Julien's condition worsened around the same time my tenant informed me that due to a transfer to another province, he had to end his lease agreement. Val advised me to leave the property vacant, and Eli agreed to keep an eye on it. Leaving it vacant also served as an escape when I needed a break from caring for Julien or when it was his children's turn to visit. It became my therapy as I cleaned and decorated to suit myself. With Donna's help, I ordered all modern appliances, indoor and outdoor furniture, and anything else I needed.

A couple of months later, the hospital recommended hospice care. The earth moved under my feet as though experiencing the seismic activity of a minor earthquake. Julien's body had a tough time fighting infections, and the advanced cirrhosis became life-threatening as more scar tissue formed, making it difficult for his liver to function properly. The end was near. The evidence was undeniable. My world began to fall apart.

The weather had just begun to turn cold when Julien progressed to unresponsiveness or coma. On an early September afternoon, I arrived at the hospital to visit with my husband. I knew Julien's health had taken a turn for the worse when his children walked past me in the hospital hallway without their normal sarcasm about my appearance or the big, low-class bags I carried. My steps quickened. I ran. My heart pounded. Blood rushed to my head.

The sun cast its last rays on the horizon when Julien took his final breath, quietly slipping away one month after my forty-fourth birthday.

Once again, grief overwhelmed me. It grew and wrapped around me like a blanket. Then it grew heavier from the stress of preparing for the funeral. Julien's children insisted that their father's final resting place be in the same cemetery as their mother's side of the family. However, much to their displeasure, I chose a cemetery on the other side of town.

But Julien's children were amateurs compared to my mother. My heart raced, and I began to panic just thinking about what my mother would say or do.

Will I die from mortification?

My shoulders grew tense, the cords in my chest tightened as I walked on shaky legs to attend the funeral service. Before entering the chapel, I looked up to observe the sun displaying its brilliance in the cloudless sky.

Just for you, my love.

Taking a deep breath, I stepped inside. Blood pounded in my ears when I noticed Julien's children sitting with their mother, across from me. Dressed all in white, they constantly sniffled loudly and wiped their eyes. My stomach churned.

Oh Lord, help me.

I prayed that my mother wouldn't attend the funeral. My heart rate slowed, and I took a long, slow, deep breath when I noticed her absence. Still, I felt an overwhelming sense of dread. I sweated. I waited with a dry throat. My mother timed her appearance perfectly. She appeared at the door a minute before the service start time. Like a movie star attending an award ceremony. I, along with all those in attendance, turned around to observe the commotion.

Oh, no!

Dressed in all black, complete with a veil over her face and a black handkerchief dangling from her left hand, my mother strolled to the front of the chapel. My head pounded. My hands shook. Then, during the service, she refused to be upstaged by the sniffles coming from Julien's children. My mother responded by making pathetic whimpering sounds.

Panic clawed at my throat, my legs grew weak, and I leaned into Val for support and to distract myself. My breathing became hard, as if I'd just returned from jogging. I groaned silently.

Please don't let me faint.

Stress overrode my grief.

When will this day end? I felt as though I was outside my body. Floating. My mind went blank, and I completely dissociated from the proceedings, from my surroundings.

• • •

At the reading of the will, the lawyer requested that I arrive before the appointed time. He handed me a duffle bag after I took a seat in the end chair, one of the four chairs arranged in a semicircle facing his desk. I peered into the bag. My heart raced. My breath came out in small gasps and my hand flew to cover my mouth. Hundred-dollar bills. Just like in the movies. I lifted my head, my eyes wide and questioning.

The lawyer responded with a smile. "Julien wanted you to have this. He said you would understand."

Minutes later, Julien's three children arrived, glaring at me before moving their chairs away as though I had a contagious disease. But I heard their snickers.

"What a joke."

CHAPTER THIRTY-TWO

"She even brings a bag to the reading."

"No class."

Enough!

I shook my head at their childish and pathetic behaviour.

I loved Julien, but I was happy never to see his children after the reading. They had slighted me when their father married me. Now that he was gone, he could no longer protect me, and I no longer cared about their existence. I now thought of them as dust—dust I wanted to brush off my shoulders. Gone and forgotten. I hoped the reading would go smoothly and shorten the time I would have to endure their presence.

In a last-ditch attempt to insult me, they wanted to contest the financial amount bequeathed to me, but the lawyer put a stop to it. "As his wife, she's legally entitled to financial support. It's either the money or the house. Your choice." As expected, the thought of losing their mother's house effectively put a stop to the arguments.

After the reading, I waited about five minutes before leaving the lawyer's office and wasn't surprised to find them waiting to ambush me outside the building. They confronted me with stony faces and crossed arms. "That money you get won't go far. We're sure you'll be looking for the next sugar daddy in no time." Their shrill laughs grated on my nerves.

Like hyenas.

"We're giving you one day to leave our mother's house. And don't take what's not yours." I shook off the dust.

I drove to the park to catch my breath. The cool air calmed me while I feasted my eyes on the warm hues of red, orange, and brown. For a moment, the beauty made me forget my grief, yet it also served to remind me that it was a season of transition, of change. It was a time in the death-to-rebirth cycle.

I sighed heavily. My husband was gone, and the daunting prospect of starting a new life lay before me. Once again, the hammer of change fell. I slowly reached for the duffle bag and held it on my lap for a few minutes before opening it. My hand automatically went to my heart. I stared at the money for a few minutes before I dared to count it. Three hundred thousand dollars.

Our emergency fund.

Silent tears ran down my face as my whisper echoed in the car. "Thank you, honey. Thank you."

CHAPTER
THIRTY-THREE

"The only way to end grief was to go through it."
—Holly Black, *The Darkest Part of the Forest*

I RETURNED TO my marital home to pack my few remaining items. Tears ran down my face as I stood outside and took one last look at the house where I'd known joy and happiness for eighteen years. I had walked through those doors as an inexperienced and insecure girl and grown into a mature woman with the protection, kindness, and support of a loving husband. Julien appeared when I was at my lowest and needed a friend. He'd brought happiness and joy into my life and opened my heart to trust and hope. I would miss him terribly.

I moved into my home after dropping off the key at the lawyer's office. I broke down the minute I walked through the door, my tears and pain for the loss of my husband and friend, for the loss of the life I knew, for everything I'd lost. Julien had understood and accepted me. Although I knew Julien had chosen me because he loved me, I became an ideal wife, hoping that he wouldn't think of me as damaged goods. And yet I loved him with my whole being.

Even though I had expected that losing Julien would hurt, I wasn't prepared for the intensity of the grief. It crushed me, catching me off guard. Unable to fight it, I surrendered to its comfort. I gave in to the depression, the pain, the grief, the loneliness, and the loss.

• • •

Voices sounded far away. "Nikki, wake up. Wake up. We're taking you to urgent care."

I groaned.

Who?

"Nikki! Nikki! Wake up."

I exercised extreme effort to open my eyes. Halfway.

Someone pulled me upright. "Donna will help you."

Eli.

With numerous pins and needles stabbing at me, it was difficult to stand, to walk. I mumbled. "Where are we going again?"

"Urgent care."

"Why?"

"Oh Nikki, you're burning up. You just don't look well. You need to see a doctor."

I was tired. Losing myself in sleep appeared more appealing than going to the doctor. He or she couldn't give me the one thing I wanted—my husband.

The drive to urgent care seemed endless. I wanted to sleep. Luckily, the wait was short. The tired-looking doctor was brief. "You have rheumatoid arthritis."

I nodded. My body tensed. There must be a million and one questions about the disease. I just couldn't think of one.

Noticing my struggle, the doctor's voice softened. "I'm prescribing medication. It will lead to a remission of your symptoms, including the swelling in your joints." Then he provided information about the disease, but nothing registered.

• • •

The following weeks were difficult and made less lonely by the support and love from family. Val phoned every day and visited weekly, sometimes bringing my father with her. Eli and Donna did my shopping, and Eli maintained everything inside and outside the house. My fridge was full to overflowing with the cooked food from Mrs. Carmen. Unfortunately, I didn't have much of an appetite and gladly shared the meals with Eli and Donna. Donna joked that Eli came just for the food.

October arrived before I was ready to think about Thanksgiving. Eli didn't ask. He simply told me I was spending Thanksgiving with his family. "I'll be here around 10:00 a.m. to pick you up."

"That's too early. Why don't you have it without me."

"No." His voice firm.

"I think it's too soon to go out. I'm still recuperating."

Still mourning.

Eli peered down at me. "Be ready when I get here." Was this big brother flexing his muscles?

I overslept that day. Unintentionally. "Sorry, Eli." My tears were close to the surface. "I'll get ready."

"I'll wait," he said, making himself comfortable.

My Thanksgiving excursion into daylight prepared me for the longer trip to Toronto for the Christmas holidays. I decided to avoid the stress of driving on the highway and took the commuter train. My week with Val, her family, and my father turned out to be the medication I needed. The food was plentiful and always available—temptations my appetite couldn't resist.

"Aunty, here's a piece of cake."

"Aunty, I made this just for you."

"Nikki, you've got to try this."

"Nikki, is there anything else I can get for you?"

"I have a special treat for my princess."

No one mentioned my mother, but I knew it wasn't in her nature to keep away. She waited four months after Julien's death to drop in unannounced. "It's months since I saw and spoke with you." She sucked her teeth. "What kind of daughter are you? I'll tell you. A daughter who couldn't even pick up the phone to call her mother for Christmas. I had to come to make sure you're okay."

I stood by, silently, as she let her gaze roam everywhere, poking her head in the fridge, peeking into the rooms before announcing, "Nice house." She huffed, unable to find fault, unable to be critical. "Seems I would die waiting for an invitation. You know George would have liked to see it."

Over my dead body.

I shifted my weight from one foot to the other, then started fidgeting with my hair and clothes. Minutes passed in silence. I wrapped my arms around my body. Marian looked at me, folded her arms, and remarked, "You had a chance to have children. Why didn't you take it? What happened? Did you tell him your little secret?"

I stared at her with no show of emotion, and without saying a word, I opened the front door for her to leave. My mother cast a displeased look at me, pulled her jacket closer to her body, lifted her head, and marched out.

CHAPTER
THIRTY-FOUR

"It's a funny thing about life, once you begin to take note
of the things you are grateful for, you begin to lose sight
of the things that you lack."
—Germany Kent

LIKE THOUGHTS OF my mother, winter didn't want to leave. However, I'd forgotten all about my mother's intrusion by the time spring rolled around. On one sunny day, my coffee forgotten, I lay curled up under a throw in the all-season sunroom, mourning the loss of my husband, when my gaze sharpened to focus on a butterfly fluttering outside for about five minutes before disappearing. I sat up, remembering the appearance of the single butterfly when Julien proposed, giving me a fresh start. Was this sighting a sign of hope, of a new beginning? I shook my head. I wasn't ready for a fresh start, but I was ready to take a shower and get out of the house.

When humans need comfort, we tend to return to what's familiar. Returning to the island was out of the question, so I chose to immerse myself in the lush tropical foliage and cascading waterfalls at the Cambridge butterfly conservatory. As I walked along the meandering pathways, the free-flying butterflies fluttered around me, allowing me to suspend thinking and free my mind, while the tropical plants and gorgeous blooms brought sunshine into my heart. The smile on my face remained long after buying a metal butterfly wind chime at the gift store.

• • •

CHAPTER THIRTY-FOUR

When I felt better, I took stock of my finances. Thanks to Julien's generosity, I had enough to maintain the house and car, but I couldn't hide forever. Still, I remained lost like a rudderless ship, drifting aimlessly, unable to find my footing, to find my direction. Questions swirled in my mind.

Am I afraid? How will I survive without Julien? Where will I start? What will I do?

It took ten months before I had the strength and courage to start looking for work.

One evening after my job search proved futile, I called Val. "I'm not having any luck getting to work as a decorator or stager with a real estate agent," I said, cringing as I heard how the flat tone in my voice reflected my frustration.

"What's their response?"

My voice broke. "Either they don't need one or they're already working with one."

"So what are you going to do?"

Sighing heavily, I mumbled. "Cleaning ... I guess. It's the only other thing I know how to do."

"Are you okay with that?"

"What do you mean?"

"Will you look at it as going backwards, or will you look at it as returning to something you excel in?"

I let her questions ruminate in my mind before answering. "Good questions. Cleaning was never beneath me. It's honest work and something I'm good at." I paused for a minute. "But I want my independence. The independence I had working with Julien."

"So where do you start?"

I chuckled. "Just talking to you gave me an idea." The pitch of my voice rose. "Instead of working for a company, what if I work for myself?"

"You would certainly have your independence. Go on."

"What if I talk to the people in my neighbourhood? There a many two-income families who could use a helping hand."

"That's great! The outside of your home is your billboard. One look and they know you do an amazing job."

My voice became animated. "Yeah! I can choose my clients. I just need a few. Working four days a week is all I need to keep me busy."

"Will they be open to you?"

"I hope so. I spent months walking the neighbourhood and greeting my neighbours. I'm no longer a stranger. Providing them with a service will be the last piece of the puzzle."

CHAPTER
THIRTY-FIVE

"There can be no hope without faith in Christ, for hope is
rooted in him alone. Faith without hope would, by itself,
be empty and futile."
—Ernst Hoffmann

FINDING A FEW clients in my neighbourhood proved easy, as most people needed the extra help. I cleaned one house per day from Mondays to Thursdays, except on holidays. I went shopping on the fifth workday, Friday, or reserved the day for self-care. One week after I started working, I walked out of the hairdresser's salon with my hair styled in braids. Flipping the braids, my steps light, I lifted my face to embrace the cool October air. On an impulse, I stopped off at a church on my way home.

A calm settled over me as I walked through the doors and into the narthex before the hushed silence of the dim, empty church greeted me. Memories flooded my mind as the familiar scents drifted to my nose. Memories of holding my aunt's hand skipping down the aisle in my Sunday best, of wrinkling my nose at the incense and singing loudly in an off-key voice.

I sat in one of the back pews and knew the time was right to do some soul searching. In the peace and quiet, I took a long, deep breath and reflected on the blessings in my life as I quieted my mind to admit that I did not get to this place on my own.

I'd made a mistake with Lucy Grant, but I recalled she was the first person to extend an olive branch to me. Although she had challenged, annoyed, stalked, and betrayed me, she was my first friend in Canada. Then Anna Landry was at my side during my darkest days. She took on the role of sister, consoler, and friend when my mother banished me and I had no one. She made me realize I was never alone, even in my darkest days. She saved me. Julien taught me the power of love, nurturing me from a naïve girl to a confident woman, and through it all, the love and support from Val, Eli, and Mrs. Carmen remained unwavering.

I leaned back in the pew with my eyes closed, remembering that when I was fourteen, I asked Jesus to carry me because of the weight of my burden, and He had granted my wish. Looking back, I must have subconsciously remembered His words: "… *I am not alone, because the Father is with me*" (John 16:32b). Those words had helped me because it seemed that in my short lifetime, I was constantly trying to climb out of the wreckage of grief and pain.

Wiping away a few tears that escaped through my closed eyes, I recalled many dark moments of discouragement and confusion, but even during the darkness, Christ had remained steady as my light, my rock.

My mindfulness helped me see God's hand in my life and allowed me to thank Him for putting the many people in my life. My tears were tears of gratitude. I sniffled, knowing I had many more lessons to learn but that I could continue my life's journey aware that although many dark days waited around the corner, hope would carry me through. I needed to grow my faith to experience the power of God in my life. Just like Peter in the scripture reading, fear would not stop me from getting out of the boat. I believed I would not falter or drown in sorrow when I focused on Him.

The following Sunday, I returned to my traditional church, hoping for brighter days. The weight of my burden lightened after looking within and cataloguing my imperfections, but it was just the first step in growing spiritually. My grief caused me to have an emotional connection with God, but I wanted a personal one chosen in faith, with the surety that the journey of faith would lead me to choose Him repeatedly.

With a beam of sunlight illuminating the cross, the words of the song "Come Back to Me (Hosea)" touched my heart in many ways: "Come back to me with all your heart. Don't let fear keep us apart."[1] Taking a deep breath,

---

[1] Gregory Norbert, "Hosea," 1972, Hymnary.org, accessed October 15, 2024, https://hymnary.org/text/come_back_to_me_with_all_your_heart.

CHAPTER THIRTY-FIVE

I closed my eyes, letting the words seep into my soul. Words that started me on the journey to forgive myself to find freedom to sleep secure in peace. *Lord, I'm a sinner. I'm living my entire life with a mistake. I also know I'm a receiver of your grace, mercy, and direction. Help me to move forward.*

● ● ●

Working through my grief allowed me to come to terms with my loss. I hadn't fully accepted it, and now I acknowledged that my helpers would always be at my side. Letting go brought on a flood of tears.

Lord, let those tears heal me.

My grief had changed over the years, and now I found myself grieving for the person my child might have become as my son. But the reality was that I had no say in his future. He was someone else's son.

> Dearest Joel,
>
> I lost my husband, Julien, recently. He was also my friend, my advisor, and my protector. In an alternate universe, he would be the perfect father, and I want to think that you would have liked him. You would have gotten along fabulously with him.
>
> Once again, I have come to a bend in the road, and I must decide which path to take and then learn to live with my choice. But I am older this time, and although the loss is hard, I don't feel as though I'm thrown into the deep, dark end of the sea with no means of surviving. Time does make a difference. Now I admit that praying and asking for help from family and friends helped me navigate the bumps along the way.
>
> You're also not here. I've lost you. But you, dear child, were never mine to lose. I put you up for adoption so that you would have a mother and father to guide you, to watch over you from childhood to adulthood. They're the ones who helped you deal with changes when you were younger and gave you the tools to manage any change as an adult.

I'm hoping life has been good to you and you met your soulmate. This is a huge, life-changing event! A joyful one. I'm excited for you. This is a turning point in your life. I hope you're lucky in love, as I am.

The years are piling up with changes. Do you have a child? I imagine you with a child of your own. Someone to give your life meaning and purpose. As the years roll on, as you deal with one change after the other, I want you to be grateful for the helping hand from your parents and from your friends. We need people to grow, to survive.

Always in my heart.

CHAPTER
THIRTY-SIX

"My scars remind me that I did indeed survive my deepest wounds. That in itself is an accomplishment. And
they bring to mind something else, too. They remind me
that the damage life has inflicted on me has, in many
places, left me stronger and more resilient. What hurt me
in the past has actually made me better equipped
to face the present."
—Steve Goodier

EIGHTEEN MONTHS AFTER my husband's death, I decided to tackle my grief head on. Since forgiving myself included making peace with my past, it didn't happen overnight. It was a gradual process that started before I met Julien. I lived with my depression for such a long time that I grew accustomed to the familiarity of keeping one foot in the past, even during my marriage. Time for a change.

Taking the first step on my spiritual journey gave me more peace and filled me with hope and confidence. I reminded myself daily to take responsibility for my mistake and fully immerse myself in the present, to laugh out loud and be grateful for the unimportant things.

I started every morning with gratitude, raised the volume on the radio, and danced while preparing my breakfast. Morning walks became my routine on my off days, and I gradually added weekly yoga and meditation classes. With a short work week, I spent more time baking and grocery shopping so that my packed lunches included more fresh fruits and vegetables, homemade breads, scones, and muffins.

I no longer blamed my thirteen-year-old self for what happened. I finally admitted that as humans, we all make mistakes, and I sat back and looked at her journey with pride. That mistake didn't push me to abuse alcohol or drugs. It didn't define me. I was who I chose to become. I forgave myself, because I knew *"as far as the east is from the west, so far has he removed our sins from us"* (Psalm 103:12).

The people in my life accepted me. Their love and support gave me the strength to reinvent myself when the course of my life changed. I repaid them by lifting my head high, by growing up, and by living a good life.

Now it gave me immense pleasure to spend more time with my favourite people. That didn't include my mother, whom I avoided like the plague. I adjusted the lightweight shawl of grief around my shoulders and increased the number of hours I volunteered at the dog rescue.

I cherished the many weekends spent with Val, who uplifted me. My sister brought joy and comfort to my life, and our late-night conversations were both supportive and amusing.

One evening, Val grew serious during one of our conversations. "Are you ready to be open to love again?"

"What? Where did that come from?"

"It's time, Nikki."

"Yeah, I guess," I said, taking a sip of tea.

I could hear Val moving around before she said, "Okay! Great! Then you should have an idea what comes next."

"Val, I have no idea what you're getting at."

"I give up!" She sighed as though talking to one of her children who remained clueless about the conversation. "It's time you start dating."

"Dating?"

"Yes. Dating. You know, putting yourself out there … into the world. You're still extremely attractive and looking better than some women in their thirties."

"Thank you for saying that, but I only dated one man, so I'm not sure how to put myself out there."

Val chuckled. "I'm talking about a different dating from when Julien courted you." She laughed out loud. "I wouldn't call it dating because you didn't know what you were doing. He did. You didn't. This time, I want you to enjoy the process. Hey! It's a different time. You can even try online dating."

"I'll see." My voice became hesitant. Even though my marriage to Julien made me more confident and taught me to be more trusting, he always encouraged me to develop a growth mindset. I was incredibly young and unworldly when I married him, but I had a willingness to learn and approached obstacles with a curious mind. I appreciated the fact that Julien didn't find it necessary to point out my faults or become impatient with my mistakes. Instead, he taught me to see those mistakes and challenges as opportunities for learning and growth.

"One more thing."

"What?"

"Last time I saw you, you were still wearing your wedding ring. At least try to remember to remove it when you go on a date."

• • •

The warmth of the sun after a couple of cloudy days in early November warmed my soul. Straightening the scarf around my neck, I pulled the leather jacket close to my body as I sprinted toward the doors of the art gallery, anticipating the blast of warm air. I shivered slightly and then shook my body, adjusting to the warmer temperature. My gaze roamed the walls. I intended to find the perfect painting for the living room. Suddenly, I heard my name.

I looked around to see the manager walking toward me. "Oh. Hi, Gavin." I hadn't seen him in a few years, and the hint of grey along his hairline made him look distinguished. He still maintained his trim build, and his erect posture made him appear taller than average.

A ghost of a smile lit up his face when he shook my hand. "I heard about your husband. I'm sorry for your loss. Please accept my sympathy."

"Thank you."

He stepped in next to me. "Is there something you were looking for? Maybe I could be of assistance."

I told him what I wanted.

"Come with me. I'll take care of you."

I nodded, finding it difficult to look away from his soft, dark, brown eyes. My heart began to race.

Later, I walked out of the gallery with a painting and a personal invitation to the next event.

CHAPTER
THIRTY-SEVEN

"Let your hopes, not your hurts, shape your future."
—Robert H. Schuller

A MONTH LATER, the low voices of the patrons reached my ears as I wandered around on my way to the gallery housing the permanent collection. I smiled at the excitement in their voices after the showing of the meditative video that brilliantly captured the magic of the artist's exhibition. Gavin Alleyne had invited me to dinner afterwards and suggested the permanent collection area as our meeting place. I smiled broadly, realizing that I eagerly looked forward to his company.

At the seafood restaurant, Gavin fiddled with the cutlery before looking at me. "I'm sorry I missed Julien's funeral."

"No need to apologize."

"I need to. Julien was one of my best customers, and I considered him a friend. He supported me when Carissa died, but I wasn't there for you. For that, I'm sorry." Gavin's wife had passed away two years before Julien.

I murmured my thanks.

"You see, it was around the time when your husband died that I found myself drowning in grief. I had to get away. My daughter, Laura, worked for the federal government in Ottawa when her mother died, so she wasn't around afterwards. Suddenly, the two most important women in my life were gone. At least Laura lived in the same province. I couldn't function, so I took a leave of absence. I wanted to be close to my only child so that I could heal enough to return to manage the art gallery."

"Did that help?"

Gavin nodded. "It did. That time allowed me to get to a place of peace and healing. It also helped to strengthen my bond with Laura. She's my everything. I couldn't imagine life without my daughter."

"I'm glad you took the time to process everything with Laura. Family support and love are critical when you lose a loved one."

"Thank you. I knew you'd understand."

I smiled. "Was it easier getting back?"

"No." Gavin sighed. "It's never easy getting back to what was. You always think of life as 'before' and 'after.' But taking the time for self-care made me stronger. Strong enough to sell the family home with Laura's blessing and move to an apartment." He paused. "Did you keep the home you shared with Julien?"

"No. I'm living in a house I renovated while married."

He exclaimed with raised eyebrows. "Really! Sounds interesting. I'm sure there's a story there. Would you mind showing it to me sometime?"

I answered without hesitation. "Not at all."

• • •

A week later, I looked at my reflection in the mirror while getting ready for another date with Gavin. Now I understood what Val meant when she indicated that dating Gavin would be a dissimilar experience. I shook my head in amazement when I thought about how my views on relationships had evolved with age and experience. I looked at the sparkling eyes in the mirror, and my lips curled upward at the thought of finding out where this relationship would lead.

I threw myself wholeheartedly into the dating process. I treasured every experience. Because I'd recently started my faith journey, I readily accepted Gavin's invitation to accompany him to church on Sundays. Our conversations, always insightful and interesting, covered diverse topics, including ones to which we could both relate.

The confident Nikki didn't hesitate to ask the tough questions. "How did you know when it was the right time to remove your wedding ring?"

CHAPTER THIRTY-SEVEN

"Interesting question. That's a tough one. I can give you an answer, but I think it's a personal decision for everyone."

"I understand."

"I took it off after two years, but a week later it was back on my finger. It was as though I'd betrayed Carissa and wanted to sever our emotional connection. I tried a couple of times afterwards with the same result. Then I woke up one Christmas morning knowing it was time. The rings are in a keepsake box for Laura. What about you?"

"Over eighteen months after I lost Julien, my sister suggested dating and reminded me to remove my ring before going out. So I gradually started removing it whenever I cleaned, then when I exercised. But all the stress disappeared when I simply moved it to my other hand," I said, raising my right hand and wriggling my fingers. "I might have made a different decision if we had children."

● ● ●

Although Gavin claimed he cooked mainly "meat and potatoes," he enjoyed the diverse cultural dishes I prepared. I got included in all social activities when Laura paid short visits to her father on the long weekends and when she spent a week with him during the Christmas holiday. It gave me pleasure to cook whatever she requested. At the end of the festive season, I sent her home with a care package that included a small black cake and a bottle of sorrel.

Yet I worried Laura would see me as an interloper and resent me. But Gavin assured me that his daughter was the one who had encouraged him to start dating. Laura also told him she remembered me visiting the art gallery and thought of me as a kind person. Now she welcomed me with open arms and embraced my family.

Over a year after I started dating Gavin, Laura invited me to her wedding in Ottawa. The perfect time for a road trip. After the ceremony, I met Chase, Laura's husband, and some of Gavin's extended family members.

Gavin also fit in perfectly with my family. He played golf with Eli, and he drove when we went to visit Val, who adored him from the start. My father immediately embraced Gavin and treated him like a son. When he mentioned that he and his late wife had eaten dinner at the Caribbean Bistro a few times, I took immense pleasure in introducing him to Mrs. Carmen and the Bistro's brunch menu. After that, most Saturday mornings found us at the Bistro, where Eli and family would sometimes join us.

Everyone conspired to keep Gavin away from my mother for about a year and a half. I waited until my mother was alone at a summer's barbecue before introducing Gavin.

"So how long have you been seeing my daughter?"

"Long enough so that I can get to meet you." My mother rewarded him with a scrutiny and raised eyebrows, but she didn't make her usual scathing remarks.

I let out the breath I didn't realize I'd been holding. When I turned to follow Gavin, my mother grabbed my arm, preventing me from taking a step in the other direction. "I like this one. Too bad you're too old to have children."

CHAPTER

THIRTY-EIGHT

"The magic of new beginnings is truly
the most powerful of them all."
—Josiyah Martin

MY MOTHER'S BACK-HANDED approval of Gavin gave me something to consider. Did I want a future with him? I called to mind the Zen Proverb: "When the student is ready, the teacher will appear." I realized that it could be referring to my life with Julien. He'd come into my life when I was ready to experience something different—when I was ready to know what the world had to offer. On one hand, the wisdom and calmness Julien brought to our marriage made my life peaceful. On the other hand, I brought vitality and enthusiasm into his, which kept him focused on his life with me and on his business. He became my teacher, motivating, encouraging, and preparing me to face the future—whatever that entailed.

Now armed with social skills and confidence, I found it exhilarating to experience new things and to thoroughly enjoy a new relationship. Did I need another teacher? Although I was ready for a change, for a second chance at happiness, I was capable of walking side by side with Gavin. Learning never ended, but this time around I wanted a partner, not a teacher.

Life taught me that even though my mistake caused me to make an unexpected turn on my road of life, God had a purpose for my pain. After many years filled with grief and secrecy, I had ended up at the place where I was supposed to be and with the person I was meant to end up with. It just took decades to get to that place. Would I finally get the reward for all my struggles? Julien had to get me to this point in my life. Then he left, giving me his blessings to start a new life.

Was I ready for a new life? I respected Gavin. He had integrity and honesty. My heart opened to his warmth and positivity. It warmed my heart when Gavin put aside his phone or stopped whatever task held his focus to give me his undivided attention whenever I spoke with him, no matter how trivial the conversation. But what endeared me to him was the fact that he listened without judging or jumping to conclusions. I followed his example and learned to be a good listener too.

• • •

Two years after starting to date Gavin, I noticed a light in my living room when we returned home after dining out. I looked at Gavin with wide eyes, my hand reaching out to clutch his. "There's someone in the house. I didn't leave the light on. What do we do? Do we call the police?"

Gavin patted my hand. "Let me check first. Do you want to stay in the car or follow me?"

"Are you kidding? What if they run out and steal the car with me in it? It happens all the time on television. Lead the way."

I followed, grabbing a fistful of his shirt at the back and passing the keys to him on the side.

"Wait. Did you hear that?"

Gavin's voice came back to me. "Do you mean the wind chimes?"

"The wind chimes. Oh! Right. Just jumpy." Sometimes I heard the butterfly wind chimes late at night, and usually two thoughts crossed my mind just before they lulled me to sleep: Julien, and an angel got her wings.

Hmmm … nothing stirred!

Gavin opened the front door. No one jumped out. I didn't hear a sound. I peered around him. My jaw dropped and my mouth formed a perfect shape like a doughnut. Two rows of flameless candles bordered a path strewn with the petals of yellow roses leading to the dining room. My hand covered the surprise sound from my mouth as I stepped from behind Gavin to follow the yellow petal road.

CHAPTER THIRTY-EIGHT

My four-person dining table, covered with a white lace tablecloth, held a wine cooler with a bottle of wine and two glasses. They were in a serving tray sprinkled with yellow petals and sitting in the middle of the table. Gavin pulled out a chair and, still speechless, I gratefully sank into it.

Gavin held my hands. "You know, months before Carissa died, she told me to find someone who would make me happy. I love you, Nikki Robinson, and you make me incredibly happy."

My dark, curly hair pulled back in a chignon left my face exposed. I smiled. My face lit up from all I felt inside. My stomach flipped and my heart thudded a bit harder when Gavin leaned into me. His low baritone voice sent delicious shivers down my spine. "Will you marry me?"

I accepted, ready for a new beginning.

• • •

We opted for a Christmas wedding, giving Laura and Chase an opportunity to attend. I gave my mother more notice this time.

She made a short, deep sound. "You finally got it right. At least I got to meet my future son-in-law before the wedding. A wedding, which I'm happy to note, is not scheduled for next month." She paused. "Do you want George to give you away?"

"George?"

Heavens no!

"Yes. My husband. George." She sucked her teeth.

"No. I've asked Daddy."

I anticipated the response by moving the phone away from my ear. "What? Are you crazy?" Anyone standing outside my front door would have heard my mother berating my father and calling him all kinds of names under the sun.

When she paused to take a breath, I asked, "Does that mean you and George will not be at the wedding?"

"What a stupid thing to say. You could have asked Eli if you didn't want George. But no, you had to go and ask that man." She hung up.

• • •

In the church, surrounded by family and friends, not forgetting my mother and George, I made my vows, taking Gavin Alleyne as my second husband. Standing tall, I wore a simple cream dress and sported short, curly hair under a cream fascinator, with a linen net mesh covering half my face.

The reception took place at the Bistro, where the guests dined at tables covered with white tablecloths. The centrepiece on each table was a white vase with a red ribbon tied around its neck, holding one red flower, one white flower, red berries, and a few pine twigs. Red candles and festive garlands adorned the head table.

Besides the many alcoholic drinks, the other options included sorrel, mauby, ginger beer, and eggnog. Codfish fritters and mini vegetable samosas were part of the appetizers. Guests could enjoy Christmas fare like roast turkey with cranberry sauce, scalloped potatoes, and stuffing; island favourites like jerk chicken, rice and peas, and plantain; and seafood like baked salmon. Dessert consisted of fruits, Caribbean black cake, and various tarts, served with tea or coffee.

CHAPTER
THIRTY-NINE

"You couldn't hide from bad things and pretend they
didn't exist, that left you with a dream world, and dream
worlds eventually crumble. You had to face the truth.
And then decide what you wanted."
—Sarah Cross

ON A COLD February day, two months after the wedding, I joined Mrs. Carmen at the Bistro to express my gratitude for the amazing treatment we'd received at our wedding reception. "I deeply appreciate all you've done for me and Gavin. I don't have the words to tell you how much we value your love and support. Thank you."

"My pleasure, honey. It's the least I could do. You're like family, and I wanted you to have a reception you would always remember. I'm happy everyone had a wonderful time."

"They did, singing praises about the food and the decorations."

"I'm glad."

I gave her a bright smile. Mrs. Carmen continued to fill me with love and always gave me a sense of belonging.

"I'm happy to see you're more relaxed and you look happy."

I smiled. "I'm happy."

She reached over and took my hands. "Good. I keep praying for your happiness. God listens. He understands and knows the hopes and fears locked in our hearts. Miracles can happen when you trust in His love."

"Thanks, Aunty."

"Can I pass on what I've learned in the short time I was married?"

I squeezed her hands again. "Of course."

Mrs. Carmen looked into my eyes. "To be truthful, I received the advice from my mother, but only followed it when our marriage started heading in the wrong direction. This started happening when I became embarrassed to discuss certain topics with my husband. It created tension and misunderstanding within our marriage, and I began to keep an emotional distance."

"Oh! I'm sorry."

She waved a hand in the air. "Thanks, dear. But that was a lifetime ago. I want you to know everyone has secrets, and some can weigh us down. But all, big and small, can have a profound effect on any marriage. So please, no matter the size, try not to keep secrets from your husband. Be honest. You'll be amazed at the difference this makes. Keeping secrets can tax you mentally and lead to suspicion, insecurity, and loneliness in a marriage. When you share your secret, you'll no longer carry a heavy burden, and it will open your heart wider for love and draw you closer as a couple."

"Thank you, Aunty."

"The words of Luke 8:17 are clear: '*For there is nothing hidden that will not become visible, and nothing secret that will not be known and come to light.*'"

Tears shimmered in my eyes.

• • •

Later that evening, I sat looking at the shoebox tied with a blue ribbon on the kitchen table.

Oh Lord, show me how to unload my emotional baggage.

I rubbed my palms together and waited.

Hours later, Gavin asked, "Why are you in the dark?" while turning on the lights.

"Oh!" I blinked. "I didn't realize it was so late."

He gave me a concerned look. "Are you okay?"

"Yes," I said, motioning for him to take a seat. "Please. Can we talk?"

Gavin sat but kept quiet, his gaze zeroing in on the box.

CHAPTER THIRTY-NINE

I untied the ribbon. "My mother once called me damaged goods, and unfortunately, I can't seem to get rid of that label. I don't want this to affect our marriage. I want you to know the baggage I'm bringing to this relationship. I want to believe I can be whole again."

I held up a hand when Gavin wanted to speak. "Please let me tell you everything first." He nodded and listened to my story, beginning with my arrival in Canada. I spoke brokenly for over two hours about my son, my struggles, and my grief. "I was in labour for twelve hours. I know because I later checked the time of birth. I had no one to hold my hand. I thought I couldn't go on."

"I'm so sorry. It must have been extremely difficult for you."

"Yes." Then I disclosed the struggles I faced with my health. Gavin listened, holding the space for me to share my grief and pain.

He glanced at the open box. "Are these all the cards and letters?"

"Oh no. They are the first letters. The others are in a storage box."

After a silence he asked, "What about the boy who hurt you?"

"What about him?"

"Have your paths ever crossed?"

"No. It was never about him."

"That's true."

Gavin held my hands after a break for a light supper. "I know how difficult it was to reveal a secret you've kept hidden for so many years. But I love you even more for telling me, for trusting me. I'll guard you with my life."

I smiled through my tears.

He continued. "I've lived with emotional baggage for many years." He chuckled at my raised eyebrows. "Even though it's over five years, I still remember how I wrestled with grief after losing Carissa to cancer. I couldn't sleep and lost my appetite. I stayed away from everyone, and after a while the phone calls dropped off. Let me tell you a few things that helped me to live life differently, some of which can help you work through yours."

Gavin's love flooded my heart and steered the ship of my soul in the direction of peace, safety, and joy. I could move forward with faith. Counselling had saved him. It had helped him move on with his life, and he recommended that I try a few sessions, even volunteering to accompany me if I so desired.

CHAPTER
FORTY

"Don't be sad dear hearts, don't burden your precious
self with regrets. Everything we do and everyone we
meet teaches us a valuable lesson along the way. Every
single experience is needed, nothing is a waste of time.
Each encounter is teaching us to become stronger, wiser
and to have faith in our own soul. Only then every step
we take will lead us to peace and freedom."
—Mimi Novic, *Guidebook to Your Heart*

I ARRIVED EARLY for my appointment with the counsellor, Simone Nadeau.
Maybe I was eager, maybe I wanted a few quiet moments before talking to a
stranger. For decades, I had wandered in the valley of suffering. Now would
everything change? I was open to change. I was vulnerable. But whatever
the reason, a calm settled over me. I closed my eyes and breathed deeply to
clear my mind. I had a five-minute wait.

I smiled, thinking that it takes a special kind of person to be a counsellor. I felt the warmth in Simone's smile, her greeting, and her handshake. She
listened as I recounted my life from the day I moved to Canada. Her eyes
were warm and kind when she spoke. "Let's talk about the sexual violence
you experienced and the impact it had on your life."

I recounted, over a few sessions, that although I was drugged during
the sexual assault, the shame and loneliness continued because the assault
created a chain reaction that led to my pregnancy, placing my baby for

adoption, and living with the secret. It became the catalyst for my depression. "All my pain merged into one, making it impossible to place the blame for the grief on any one hurt. Then I found myself submerged in a sea of darkness, with the depression undulating like waves. I used all my energy trying to keep afloat, trying to find the light, looking for hope. Always fighting depression."

Simone observed, "That's a long time to be burdened with a secret. But you decided to reveal the secret to your husband. Can you tell me why?"

"I'm tired of secrets. I want an open and transparent marriage."

"Did you want anything else from him?" she asked with a gentle voice.

"I think I wanted his support."

"Good. You love him and you wanted his support. What about your other family members. Do you have their support?"

"My sister supports me. My brother and father don't know what happened."

"Anyone else?"

"My mother," I answered, crossing my arms over my chest.

Although Simone's expression remained neutral, she said, "I see. Take your time. Mothers and daughters can sometimes have a complex relationship. Tell me about yours."

The words were waiting to be released. They poured out, with the thickness of syrup, from my heart. "My mother has never acknowledged my loss."

Simone's words consoled me. "You were what? Fourteen. Far too young to have acquired the ego strength necessary to grieve in an unsupported environment. Your grieving process was impeded without the support from those closest to you."

"I'm glad you said that. But what about all the health problems I started to experience afterwards?"

"That's because you suppressed your grief. Your body reacted accordingly."

"How else did my body react?" I asked.

"Have you heard of postpartum depression?"

"Yes. Did I have that? Could that explain why I developed mood swings, causing me to be exhausted and more confused?"

"Yes. It could also have magnified your shame and self-loathing."

"Now I know I wasn't as far gone as I thought. Even though I cried a lot when I put my baby up for adoption, it was the depression that caused me to have crying spells and experience grief and sadness."

Simone explained further. "Sometimes the depression is sadness muddled up with irritation and a general inability to manage in the ordinary world. There's also a feeling of worthlessness and failure, and an inability to concentrate. Sometimes it's like everything leaves you feeling inexplicably flat. Sometimes even a simple task can be overwhelming."

At the end of our sessions, my perspective shifted. The teenage life experiences made me question whether I was enough. I now know that my struggle with grief was real, it was human, and I was worthy of love and belonging: "*I have the strength for everything through him who empowers me*" (Philippians 4:13).

Furthermore, talking with Simone helped me move forward in the grieving process. Gavin was right when he assured me the sessions would allow me to see that grief and pain for a birth mother placing her baby for adoption were normal.

I remembered that my life would never be the same after I found out I was pregnant at age fourteen. My life had veered off track, and the future became unimaginable. But the counselling sessions confirmed what I already knew—that my pain, shame, and grief had moulded me into a new person.

After talking to Gavin and the counsellor, part of my heart was still missing and would always be missing, but I was at peace. Was it worth the risk I took to be vulnerable and find love with Julien and Gavin? That was a resounding yes. It was a day-to-day struggle, but I lived courageously after putting up my baby for adoption, and I allowed myself to fully experience the feelings of loss, sadness, and grief.

It took years of crying rivers of tears, bearing the burden of grief, berating myself with shame, and harbouring a secret before I could begin to unpack and relinquish the heavy load I carried. With help from Gavin and the counsellor, I finally responded to Jesus's invitation to come to Him.

I also had to consider what He wanted me to learn through my marriages about myself, about relationships, about openness to life, and about surrendering to His will. I had to open my heart wider and trust Him more fully. It still hurt, but Jesus's presence gave me peace. And it made all the difference knowing I never walked alone. I was finally in a safe place to be held, to let go and be loved. Finally, I walked across the threshold of hope.

• • •

It took years for me to learn to live with my absent child.

My Dearest Joel,

The world is made up of several types of people. People like my mother, who are more concerned with public opinion than with the mental health of those close to her; people like Brian, who prey on the insecure so that they can be seen as a big person in the eyes of those who worship them; inexperienced people like me, whose needs become exploited by those with power; people like Mrs. Carmen and my sister, who recognize the wounded and become their advocate and support them wholeheartedly; and people like Julien and Gavin, who love, support, and encourage their partner to grow and find freedom.

Over the decades, I wondered, imagined, and hoped that you became a person with integrity, a kind and generous man, and that with love and support you became a man who reached down to lift those less fortunate than you. Yet my greatest hope was that a loving couple adopted you and provided the environment you needed to grow and thrive.

That hope brings me peace.

However, you're the part of me that will be forever missing, and I've come to accept that and know that that too is okay.

That's what healing looks like for me.

Always in my heart.

CHAPTER
FORTY-ONE

"We all have battles to fight. And it's often in those battles that we are most alive: it's on the frontlines of our lives that we earn wisdom, create joy, forge friendships, discover happiness, find love, and do purposeful work."
— Eric Greitens, *Resilience*

THE LOVE AND support from my family and the safe spaces from my husband and counsellor where I could be open about my pain and grief mended my soul and put the bloom on my physical body. I was like a cracked vase with gold filling in the break lines, making the new vase even more valuable and more beautiful. My cracks made me more empathetic, more open to everyone, and they made me the person who could look at her reflection in the mirror and smile. According to James Baldwin, "Not everything that is faced can be changed, but nothing can be changed until it is faced."[2] I was enough. Finally.

I was ready for God to transform my good life into a fully alive human life. His love for me was present when I went to the darkest parts of my heart at age fourteen and just as present as it was on the mountaintop moments when I married Julien and Gavin.

---

[2] "James Baldwin Quotes," Goodreads, accessed November 5, 2024, https://www.goodreads.com/quotes/14374-not-everything-that-is-faced-can-be-changed-but-nothing.

The Lord gave me a loving, caring spouse in Gavin, and a life that mattered and would have great positive consequences. Love became the anchor in our marriage and in our faith. Love held us in place when we struggled or faced challenges and temptations. Both our earthly love and our divine love fortified us for the future and enriched our souls so we could help others. *"We know that all things work for good for those who love God, who are called according to his purpose"* (Romans 8:28).

• • •

One evening after Gavin returned from volunteering at the regional food bank, he surprised me by asking, "I had this brainwave. What do you think of the idea of us doing something to serve the community?"

"But that's what you're doing. And you're also a Eucharistic minister at church. Isn't that enough?"

Gavin chuckled. "That's what I'm doing. But I want us to do something together."

"Like what?"

"I have an idea after meeting and talking to a lot of young people at the food bank."

"So you want us to help young people. How?"

"We can start a youth group for at-risk boys and girls. We can brainstorm what we need to accomplish, what we need to focus on, the name, the structure, finances, stuff like that. What do you think?"

"It's a great idea, but I don't think I have anything to offer."

"Just the opposite. You're the perfect person. You'll understand what they're going through. You've walked in their shoes."

"Yeah. But won't they question the fact that I didn't go to college?"

"Come here." Wrapping his arms around me, Gavin reassured me. "All the kids need is someone who will listen to them, give them a safe space, and force them to look at the choices they're making. They don't necessarily need a person with a college degree. They need a caring person. They need you."

Taking our inspiration from Matthew 13:3–8, we decided to use the name Transformers. Not only would they identify with the name, but we hoped to provide the youths with rich soil in which their self-confidence and faith would take root and create opportunities for them to see themselves as agents of transformative change in their lives.

• • •

Experiencing freedom from the heavy weight of shame and grief made it possible for our marriage to blossom and made me look at those in my life with fresh eyes. It gave me the strength to empathize with teens who needed support and guidance. I ended 2019 on a high note, looking forward with considerable expectations to the new year.

However, the new year started in a sustained climate of fear from COVID-19 as uncertainty took over the entire world. Businesses closed, and everyone entered a lockdown period. People had to rethink their way of life, their values, and their priorities. Gavin and I used the isolation time for self-reflection and grew closer in our marriage. I concluded that during the decades of stillness, the Lord kept fighting for me and preparing to answer my prayer. *"The Lord will fight for you; you have only to keep still"* (Exodus 14:14).

CHAPTER
FORTY-TWO

*"Blessed is the man who perseveres in temptation, for
when he has been proven he will receive the crown of life
that he promised to those who love him"* (James 1:12).

IN 2022, THE world began to shake off the restrictions imposed during the pandemic. After two years, people started to travel again, to socialize with more people and return to work. Change. During the lockdown period, Gavin had lost one of his employees to the coronavirus, forcing him to take a good look at his health and priorities. He made the choice to retire, returning to his first love—photography. I decided to stop working, and after the dog rescue re-opened, I returned as a volunteer. New beginnings.

But the isolation left its mark in other ways. We had made the decision to keep supporting the youth by connecting with them online, and they returned in larger numbers when we gradually returned to in-person meetings. Gavin and I found that the coronavirus had a negative impact on the mental health and well-being of adolescents, young people, and adults, thus demonstrating the necessity of social support and social interactions. We adjusted accordingly, tailoring our programs to help our youth manage their frustration, stress, and confusion.

● ● ●

Change lurked around every corner. I was fifty-three years old when I received an email from an unknown person. The subject line mentioned receiving my contact information from a close family friend. After opening the email, I read a few lines and then blinked. My jaw dropped, my heart skipped a beat, and my hand covered my mouth. "What? How?" I pushed my chair away from the desk and shouted, "Gavin! Gavin!"

Gavin rushed to my side. "What's wrong? Are you okay?"

Words failed me, so I pointed to the computer.

Gavin knelt at my side after reading the email. "This is from an adoption consultant. Do you know what this means?"

I shook my head, afraid to speak.

"I would guess that your son is trying to find you."

My eyes filled with tears while my hand rested on my heart. "I don't know."

"You don't know if you want him to find you, or you don't know if you want to get to know him?"

"Yes. No." I shook my head. "Yes. It's my lifelong wish. My lifelong prayer. But I'm scared of taking that step."

"Why?"

"What if he blames me? What if he hates me?"

"He's trying to find you, so I don't think he hates you."

My curiosity prompted a search that revealed that the role of an adoption consultant was to help reunite adoptees with their biological families and to help birth mothers connect with their children. My secret was a secret no more. Gavin encouraged me to respond.

I counted every second of every day after clicking the send button. Gavin refrained from making any comment when I checked and spoke to my computer every hour. "Come on, come on. Email where are you? What will you tell me … about my son?"

An email appeared in my inbox early in April. I became paralyzed and excited at the same time. I moved to the window to boost my inner strength. Winter slowly gave way to spring as new life started to emerge from the ground, and buds appeared on the trees. The time had come. My fingers trembled. A miracle in the highest order was about to unfold in my life. One email and the secrets, the unknown, the fear, the guilt, the darkness would all tumble out. There was no going back. It was time to pull back the curtain. What was once hidden was about to become known.

CHAPTER FORTY-TWO

I let the tears flow as I gently touched the screen. The beat of my heart was so loud that I was certain Gavin heard it. The email came from Connor. My son's name was Connor Taylor. A few words and phrases jumped out at me as I nervously first scanned the email: "Search … birth mother … not intruding … hope."

He doesn't hate me.

I took a deep breath and exhaled. His words registered, touching every bit of my stress, rejuvenating my cells, and cleansing away the remaining sadness in my heart. My heart rate slowed, allowing me to read and reread the email in what seemed a hundred times.

Gavin teased me. "Do you know every word by heart now?"

In response, I placed a hand to my chest. "I don't have to worry, Gavin. He isn't blaming me. He just wants to get to know me. That's all." Tears filled my eyes.

Gavin kissed my forehead. "Then you'll have no trouble finding the right words to respond."

I had practice writing numerous letters to Joel. Now faced with reality, excitement and hope bubbled within me as I wrote my first email to Connor. "There are no words to describe the emotions I feel writing to you. I hoped … I longed to know that a couple adopted you, that they loved you. Tell me about your parents. Tell me about yourself." I wanted to know everything, but I didn't want to overwhelm him.

Next email.

Connor wrote that a mixed couple living in Burlington, Ontario, had adopted him. However, he was an only child. His father, an American, had protested his country's involvement in the Vietnam War. Although he was a university student, he came from a poor family with no political connections, and as a Black person, getting the family doctor to give him a medical deferment was an impossibility. He had no choice but to flee north to Canada, with the blessings of his family.

Years later, his father had married a Canadian and they settled outside of Toronto. After years of trying, they couldn't have children, and since they couldn't adopt a White child, they had a long wait to get a Black child.

Connor included pictures of his family. The pictures showed my son as a tall young man with dark, curly hair. "I'm married with two children ages six and four. Can you tell me about your family. I would love to meet them. Is summer too soon?"

I was like the bottle of soda that someone had shaken before opening. Everything exploded. Everything tingled. Colours became vivid. The sun shimmered, and my feet didn't touch the ground. The grin on my face remained fixed as my fingers skipped across the keyboard. "I have no other children." I mentioned Val, Eli, their families, and my parents. "Summer is perfect." My heart swelled.

I will never be able to sleep!

CHAPTER
FORTY-THREE

"Everything which is done in the present, affects the
future by consequence, and the past by redemption."
—Paulo Coelho

THE SECRETS WE keep always find a way of crawling up to the surface. I
had to reveal my decades-old secret to the rest of the family. Because of the
coronavirus, my mother preferred to limit her contact to family members. I
chose to visit her on a Sunday afternoon, knowing she would be a challenge.

"Mama, do you remember the baby, my son, I placed for adoption?"

"I didn't know it was a boy." She shrugged unconcerned. "What about
him?"

"My son made contact with me, and we plan to meet in summer."

"You what? Are you crazy? I thought you had buried that … that business years ago. The past is in the past. Why do you want to bring it up
now?" She stood up and glared at me. "Haven't you heard the expression:
let sleeping dogs lie? Believe me, you're just going to make things worse.
For Pete's sake. You have a husband. Why can't you leave well alone and
let it go?" And with that, she stormed out of the room. I heard the bedroom
door slam shut.

I sat in the car with my head resting on the steering wheel. My love for
my mother always left me conflicted. I loved her and I hated her, but I was at
peace with the contradiction.

• • •

My sister agreed to host an afternoon tea so that I could break the news to my father and brother. I looked at the faces in front of me and my courage almost deserted me. Val touched my shoulder. "Nikki has something important to tell you. Please hear her out."

"Thanks, Val." I took a deep breath. "This is difficult, so let me get through it before you ask questions." They nodded. I told them my story, starting from my first day at school and ending with the communication from my son. They sat in shocked silence before asking questions and offering support. After the reveal, I felt lighter as the weight fell off my shoulders.

Tears ran down my father's face. "Oh my baby girl. It's all my fault. I'm so sorry. Sorry that I wasn't there to help you. Sorry that you had to bear that burden for all these years. But I'm here for you now. Thank you for trusting us."

Val turned to Eli. "We're sorry, Eli, for keeping you in the dark all these years. But it was my decision. We knew you would do anything to protect Nikki and punish the boy. Any action you took would have landed you in prison. We didn't want that for you. I hope you can forgive us."

Eli grew quiet. "Of course. I forgive both of you. But you're right. I would have torn the school apart looking for the scoundrel. Now everything makes sense. No sweat, Nikki. You know I've got your back."

• • •

I had to summon up my courage to tell Mrs. Carmen. How would she react? She had always shone a light in my life.

"You look troubled. Is there something I can help you with?"

"I want to thank you for the advice you gave me about not bringing secrets into the marriage." Mrs. Carmen nodded, allowing me to continue. "That's what I want to talk to you about." I stopped, unsure of my next words.

"It's okay, dear. Go on."

"Do you remember when soon after I met you, I disappeared for months, and my mother told everyone it was because I had problems adjusting and started acting up at home?"

She nodded. "Yes."

CHAPTER FORTY-THREE

I took a deep breath. "That wasn't true." Mrs. Carmen raised her eyebrows but kept silent. "I was sent to a home to keep my pregnancy a secret. I was only fourteen. I stayed there until the birth of my son, and then I put him up for adoption."

She reached for my hands. "Oh my dear child. I'm so sorry. What a burden you had to bear as a child and carry with you all your life."

"Thank you."

"What's changed?"

"My son contacted me and wants to meet soon. Aunty, I would like you to meet him. Are you okay with doing so?"

"It will be my honour, dear. Thank you."

• • •

The truth did set me free. I realized that there was a purpose for my painful past with shame and grief. I couldn't change the past, but I was thankful, because in the trial of my pain I found my purpose. I looked forward and trusted God. Now the time had come when I could walk in my destiny.

I had reached "eventually"—the day that love settled in my heart and allowed me to coast on the smooth road of peace, security, and happiness.

A line from one of my favourite musicals, *Les Misérables*, kept coming to mind: "Those who fall must pay the price." I did pay the price. But then another line said that to love another person is to see the face of God. But the way you carry your cross and live your life can have unforeseen benefits. I had finally redeemed myself.

CHAPTER
FORTY-FOUR

"No, this is not the beginning of a new chapter in my
life; this is the beginning of a new book! That first book
is already closed, ended, and tossed into the seas; this
new book is newly opened, has just begun!"
—C. Joybell

MY ANTICIPATION PREVENTED me from sleeping for days before the meeting. I remembered years earlier the excitement I felt when I received the invitation to the end-of-school party two months before my fourteenth birthday. That so-called party had changed the trajectory of my life. Now this meeting during my birthday month would be the change to bring the circle to a close.

Gavin finally took matters into his hands. He suggested that putting my feelings in one last letter might lessen my anxiety, and making an appointment with the hairdresser might give my confidence a boost. "Then you have to decide what you're going to do with the forty unaddressed birthday cards and numerous letters."

Dear Connor,

Never in a million years did I think my fourteen-year-old self would have believed that her future self would meet the child she loved and lost. I don't think she could even imagine meeting him face to face.

I thought of you every day. I saw your reflection every time I looked in the mirror. I was always fearful that you would blame me for placing you for adoption. In hindsight, I realize that I made a mistake of trusting the wrong person. A person who took advantage of my inexperience and insecurity. He was callous, shallow, and full of himself. Although I knew I had to put you up for adoption, I still spent many years wondering how you turned out and hoping that you were healthy, happy, and the antithesis of your father.

It has taken me forty years to come to this place with peace in my heart. For most of these years I've lived like a robot, struggling with the shame and guilt of abandoning you. They were years of dark moments of pain and grief when I had to keep your existence a secret.

I always thought that because I failed to live up to my mother's expectations, my future would be one of buried secrets, lies, and unhealthy living. Her decision sent me into a tailspin of despair and depression, damaging me in a way that left me scared and broken for decades. I had desperately wanted her to be happy for me, to understand what I was going through, to support me. However, with friends, other family members, and a good counsellor, I remembered that all our sins and mistakes are forgiven at the cross. I've learned that with time, hope, and the love of God, the storms of life always end. I'm living the life God intended for me to live.

Days, months, years, and decades came and went as I prayed for what seemed a hopeless intention—to know that you had a loving mother and father. Then God moved this year!

The past few months brought me unexpected hope with the reminder that darkness always comes before the dawn. The worse day of my life was forever etched in my heart as March 14, 1982. I lived with a hole in my heart for forty years. But the best day of my life, bar none, will be August 20, 2022.

Thank you for suggesting that we meet one-on-one first before you get to meet other family members.

Always in my heart.

Nikki

• • •

In the dawn of the new day, I knew the door to my heart would be wide open with this meeting. It would let in the rays of God's merciful grace, and then God would do the rest.

Gavin touched my arm and asked for the third time. "Are you sure you don't want me to go with you?"

"I'm sure. Thanks, hon. But this is something I must do by myself. You'll get to meet Connor and his family at the barbecue my sister is hosting later this afternoon."

"Okay. You look lovely. I love you."

• • •

I ran my fingers through the curls in my hair as I stepped out of the car and walked slowly toward the restaurant. No more mourning for what had happened in my past. My body hummed with excitement. The sun warmed my skin, making me appear ten years younger in the beautiful yellow and white sundress I'd recently purchased for the occasion. I glowed and dazzled like the surface of the Caribbean Sea, obliterating the cracks underneath from years of grief and pain. As I pushed open the door, my eyes zeroed in on the table to the right. A young man with a light-brown complexion stood up. My eyes widened. It was as if I'd conjured up the face of Grandpa Joel.

I blinked. The image disappeared, and I looked at the face of my adult son for the first time. I saw my son, and there was an immediate connection. We stood, transfixed, looking at each other for what seemed an eternity.

Dawn had come. Night had faded. Sadness disappeared. Joy bubbled up within me. It took forty years for the chains that shackled me to grief, guilt, and shame to break and fall off. Peace entered my heart. Forty years later, the unexplainable peace still anchored me as I clung to nothing but

CHAPTER FORTY-FOUR

God's presence near my still-aching and healing heart.

My heart expanded with a boundless love.

A warm and gentle smile bloomed across my face, breaking the spell, as I stepped forward to embrace my child for the first time.

HEALING

All choices result in consequences.
Some positive, some negative.
Although an action or decision
may not be deliberate or intentional,
there is still a price to pay.

The wrong choice can lead to pain,
to heavy hearts, broken hearts
forever scarred and stuck
living with secrets in the dark
unable to find a path to healing.

Guilt sets in after the pain,
when we hurt ourselves, family, and friends.
Often, it's a struggle to forgive,
to move past the hurt and the pain
to find the strength and courage to heal.

Look to the One who heals the deepest hurt,
who will show the way to forgiveness,
to move on with freedom from a broken past
scarred with pain and sorrow, shame, and guilt,
to find healing and to obtain closure.

ACKNOWLEDGEMENTS

THIS STORY FOUND me during the Christmas holidays, and it could only be by Divine intervention. For that, I'm profoundly grateful.

A resounding word of thanks to my review team members: Adrienne Lucas, Amah Harris, Arthur Francis, Glynis Belec, Juliet Cole, Marie-José Edwards. I can always depend on you to tell me the unfiltered truth. You're the wind beneath my wings.

The "before" and "after" life for every woman who had to put up her baby for adoption is different yet similar. Although Nikki's story is fictional, her story is their story. I can't fully express my gratitude to the woman who suggested that I use her story to inspire other women. It took a lot of courage and strength to make that decision, and I want to applaud her. I hope the story captures not only the pain and suffering she and other women experienced before meeting her child, but also the healing, peace, and joy in the end. It's a journey many women aren't strong enough to make, a journey in which the outcome can be unpredictable. It's never an easy journey no matter which road you take. Thank you.

To my editor, Linda Jenkins, for pushing me to produce a better body of work, thank you.

Thank you to my readers. I hope you enjoy this story and remember the many women who suffer in silence—women who smile while their hearts break in the struggle to live with the pain of their absent child.

ABOUT THE AUTHOR

ANGELA C. CHARLES was born in the Commonwealth of Dominica and taught high school in the Caribbean. She graduated from the University of Windsor in Ontario, Canada with a BA in Economics. She worked primarily in the banking and insurance sectors as an Information Technology Consultant in Canada and the United States. As a keen entrepreneur, Angela owned several small businesses and real estate holdings.

Angela is the author of *When God Is Silent* and *Sisi's Journey*, which was shortlisted in three categories for the 2022 Word Guild Award. Her last novel, *His Perfect Timing*, won the 2024 Word Guild Award in the "Romance" category and in the "Writer of Colour" category. She enjoys travelling and reading, and volunteers at her church and with community organizations.

Angela lives in Burlington, Ontario, Canada. You can visit her on Instagram @acharles05, on Facebook.com/Angela C Charles, or on her website www.angelacharlesauthor.com.